Mary Higgins Clark is the author of twenty-two international bestsellers. She lives with her husband, John Conheeney, in Saddle River, New Jersey.

By Mary Higgins Clark

MARY HIGGINS CLARK

POCKET
BOOKS

Silent Night

A NOVEL

POCKET
BOOKS

LONDON · SYDNEY · NEW YORK · TOKYO · SINGAPORE · TORONTO

First published in Great Britain by Simon & Schuster UK Ltd, 1995
First published by Pocket Books, 1996
This edition first published by Pocket Books, 1999
An imprint of Simon & Schuster UK Ltd
A Viacom Company

3 5 7 9 10 8 6 4 2

Simon & Schuster UK Ltd
Africa House
64-78 Kingsway
London WC2B 6AH

Simon & Schuster Australia
Sydney

A CIP catalogue record for this book is available from the British Library

ISBN 0-671-03777-3

Printed and bound in Great Britain by
Omnia Books Ltd, Glasgow

Acknowledgments

This story began when my editors, Michael V. Korda and Chuck Adams, over dinner started musing about the possibility of a suspense story set on Christmas Eve in Manhattan. I became intrigued.

Many thanks for that initial discussion and all the wonderful help along the way, Michael and Chuck.

My agent, Eugene Winick, and my publicist, Lisl Cade, offered constant support and help. Merci and grazie, Gene and Lisl.

And finally many thanks to the readers who are kind enough to look forward to my books. I wish all of you a blessed, happy, and safe holiday season.

For Joan Murchison Broad,
and in memory of Col. Richard L. Broad,
with love and thanks for all the
marvelous times we shared.

St. Christopher, patron of travelers,
pray for us, and protect us from evil.

1

It was Christmas Eve in New York City. The cab slowly made its way down Fifth Avenue. It was nearly five o'clock. The traffic was heavy and the sidewalks were jammed with last-minute Christmas shoppers, homebound office workers, and tourists anxious to glimpse the elaborately trimmed store windows and the fabled Rockefeller Center Christmas tree.

It was already dark, and the sky was becoming heavy with clouds, an apparent confirmation of the forecast for a white Christmas. But the blinking lights, the sounds of carols, the ringing bells of sidewalk Santas, and the generally jolly mood of the crowd gave an appropriately festive Christmas Eve atmosphere to the famous thoroughfare.

Catherine Dornan sat bolt upright in the back of the cab, her arms around the shoulders of her two small sons. By the rigidity she felt in their bodies, she knew her mother had been right. Ten-year-old Michael's surliness and seven-year-old Brian's silence were sure signs that both boys were intensely worried about their dad.

Earlier that afternoon when she had called her mother from the hospital, still sobbing despite the fact that Spence Crowley, her husband's old friend and doctor, assured her that Tom had come through the operation better than expected, and even suggested that the boys visit him at seven o'clock that night, her mother had spoken to her firmly: "Catherine, you've got to pull yourself together," she had said. "The boys are so upset, and you're not helping. I think it would be a good idea if you tried to divert them for a little while. Take them down to Rockefeller Center to see the tree, then out to dinner. Seeing you so worried has practically convinced them that Tom will die."

This isn't supposed to be happening, Catherine thought. With every fiber of her being she wanted to undo the last ten days, starting with that terrible moment when the phone rang and the call came from St. Mary's Hospital. "Catherine, can you come right over? Tom collapsed while he was making his rounds."

Her immediate impression had been that there had to be a mistake. Lean, athletic, thirty-eight-year-old men don't collapse. And Tom always joked that pediatricians had birthright immunization to all the viruses and germs that arrived with their patients.

But Tom didn't have immunization from the leukemia that necessitated immediate removal of his grossly enlarged spleen. At the hospital they told her that he must have been ignoring warning signs for months. And I was too stupid to notice, Catherine thought as she tried to keep her lip from quivering.

She glanced out the window and saw that they were passing the Plaza Hotel. Eleven years ago, on her twenty-third birthday, they'd had their wedding reception at the Plaza. Brides are supposed to be nervous, she thought. I wasn't. I practically ran up the aisle.

Ten days later they'd celebrated little Christmas in Omaha, where Tom had accepted an appointment in the prestigious pediatrics unit of the hospital. We bought that crazy artificial tree in the clearance sale, she thought, remembering how Tom had held it up and said, "Attention Kmart shoppers . . ."

This year, the tree they'd selected so carefully was still in the garage, its branches roped together. They'd decided to come to New York for the surgery. Tom's best friend, Spénce Crowley, was now a prominent surgeon at Sloan-Kettering.

Catherine winced at the thought of how upset she'd been when she was finally allowed to see Tom.

The cab pulled over to the curb. "Okay, here, lady?"

"Yes, fine," Catherine said, forcing herself to sound cheerful as she pulled out her wallet. "Dad and I brought you guys down here on Christmas Eve five years ago. Brian, I know you were too small, but Michael, do you remember?"

"Yes," Michael said shortly as he tugged at the handle on the door. He watched as Catherine peeled a five from the wad of bills in her wallet. "How come you have so much money, Mom?"

"When Dad was admitted to the hospital yesterday, they made me take everything he had in his billfold except a few dollars. I should have sorted it out when I got back to Gran's."

She followed Michael out onto the sidewalk and held the door open for Brian. They were in front of Saks, near the corner of Forty-ninth Street and Fifth Avenue. Orderly lines of spectators were patiently waiting to get a close-up look at the Christmas window display. Catherine steered her sons to the back of the line. "Let's see the windows, then we'll go across the street and get a better look at the tree."

Brian sighed heavily. This was some Christmas! He hated standing in line—for anything. He decided to play the game he always played when he wanted time to pass quickly. He would pretend he was already where he wanted to be, and tonight that was in his dad's room in the hospital. He could hardly wait to see his dad, to give him the present his grandmother had said would make him get well.

Brian was so intent on getting on with the evening that when it was finally their turn to get up close to the windows, he moved quickly, barely noticing the scenes of whirling snowflakes and dolls and elves and animals dancing and singing. He was glad when they finally were off the line.

Then, as they started to make their way to the corner to cross the avenue, he saw that a guy with a violin was about to start playing and people were gathering around him. The air suddenly was filled with the sound of "Silent Night," and people began singing.

Catherine turned back from the curb. "Wait, let's listen for a few minutes," she said to the boys.

Brian could hear the catch in her throat and knew that she was trying not to cry. He'd hardly ever seen Mom cry until that morning last week when someone phoned from the hospital and said Dad was real sick.

Cally walked slowly down Fifth Avenue. It was a little after five, and she was surrounded by crowds of last-minute shoppers, their arms filled with packages. There was a time when she might have shared their excitement, but today all she felt was achingly tired. Work had been so difficult. During the Christmas holidays people wanted to be home, so most of the patients in the hospital had been either depressed or difficult. Their bleak expressions reminded her vividly of her own depression over the last two Christmases, both of them spent in the Bedford correctional facility for women.

She passed St. Patrick's Cathedral, hesitating only a moment as a memory came back to her of her grandmother taking her and her brother Jimmy there to see the crèche. But that was twenty years ago; she had been ten, and he was six. She wished fleetingly she could go back to that time, change things, keep the bad things from happening, keep Jimmy from becoming what he was now.

Even to *think* his name was enough to send waves of fear coursing through her body. Dear God, make him leave me alone, she prayed. Early this morning, with Gigi clinging to her, she had answered the angry pounding on her door to find Detective Shore and another officer who said he was Detective Levy standing in the dingy hallway of her apartment building on East Tenth Street and Avenue B.

"Cally, you putting up your brother again?" Shore's eyes had searched the room behind her for signs of his presence.

The question was Cally's first indication that Jimmy had managed to escape from Riker's Island prison.

"The charge is attempted murder of a prison guard," the detective told her, bitterness filling his voice. "The guard is in critical condition. Your brother shot him and took his uniform. This time you'll spend a lot more than fifteen months in prison if you help Jimmy to escape. Accessory after the fact the second time around, when you're talking attempted murder—or murder—of a law officer. Cally, they'll throw the book at you."

"I've never forgiven myself for giving Jimmy money last time," Cally had said quietly.

"Sure. And the keys to your car," he reminded her. "Cally, I warn you. Don't help him *this* time."

"I won't. You can be sure of that. And I did not know what he had done before." She'd watched as their eyes again shifted past her. "Go ahead," she had cried. "Look around. He isn't here. And if you want to put a tap on my phone, do that, too. I want you to hear me tell Jimmy to turn himself in. Because that's all I'd have to say to him."

But surely Jimmy *won't* find me, she prayed as she threaded her way through the crowd of shoppers and sight-seers. Not this time. After she had served her prison sentence, she took Gigi from the foster home. The social worker had located the tiny apartment on East Tenth Street and gotten her the job as a nurse's aide at St. Luke's–Roosevelt Hospital.

This would be her first Christmas with Gigi in two years! If only she had been able to afford a few decent presents for her, she thought. A four-year-old kid should have her own new doll's carriage, not the battered hand-me-down Cally'd been forced to get for her. The coverlet and pillow she had bought wouldn't hide the shabbiness of the carriage. But maybe she could find the guy who was selling dolls on the street around here last week. They were only eight dollars, and she remembered that there was even one that looked like Gigi.

She hadn't had enough money with her that day, but the guy said he'd be on Fifth Avenue between Fifty-seventh and Forty-seventh Streets on Christmas Eve, so she had to find him. O God, she prayed, let them arrest Jimmy before he hurts anyone else. There's something wrong with him. There always has been.

Ahead of her, people were singing "Silent Night." As she got closer, though, she realized that they weren't actually carolers, just a crowd around a street violinist who was playing Christmas tunes.

". . . Holy infant, so tender and mild . . ."

Brian did not join in the singing, even though "Silent Night" was his favorite and at home in Omaha he was a member of his church's children's choir. He wished he was there now, not in New York, and that they were getting ready to trim the Christmas tree in their own living room, and everything was the way it had been.

He liked New York and always looked forward to the summer visits with his grandmother. He had fun then. But he didn't like this kind of visit. Not on Christmas Eve, with Dad in the hospital and Mom so sad and his brother bossing him around, even though Michael was only three years older.

Brian stuck his hands in the pockets of his jacket. They felt cold even though he had on his mittens. He looked impatiently at the giant Christmas tree across the street, on the other side of the skating rink. He knew that in a minute his mother was going to say, "All right. Now let's get a good look at the tree."

It was so tall, and the lights on it were so bright, and there was a big star on top of it. But Brian didn't care about that now, or about the windows they had just seen. He didn't want to listen to the guy playing the violin, either, and he didn't feel like standing here.

They were wasting time. He wanted to get to the hospital and watch Mom give Dad the big St. Christopher medal that had saved Grandpa's life when he was a soldier in World War II. Grandpa had worn it all through the war, and it even had a dent in it where a bullet had hit it.

Gran had asked Mom to give it to Dad, and even though she had almost laughed, Mom had promised but said, "Oh, Mother, Christopher was only a myth. He's not considered a saint anymore, and the only people he helped were the ones who sold the medals everybody used to stick on dashboards."

Gran had said, "Catherine, your father believed it helped him get through some terrible battles, and that is all that matters. He believed and so do I. Please give it to Tom and have faith."

Brian felt impatient with his mother. If Gran believed that Dad was going to get better if he got the medal, then his mom had to give it to him. He was positive Gran was right.

". . . *sleep in heavenly peace.*" The violin stopped playing, and a woman who had been leading the singing held out a basket. Brian watched as people began to drop coins and dollar bills into it.

His mother pulled her wallet out of her shoulder bag and took out two one-dollar bills. "Michael, Brian, here. Put these in the basket."

Michael grabbed his dollar and tried to push his way through the crowd. Brian started to follow him, then noticed that his mother's wallet hadn't gone all the way down into her shoulder bag when she had put it back. As he watched, he saw the wallet fall to the ground.

He turned back to retrieve it, but before he could pick it up, a hand reached down and grabbed it. Brian saw that the hand belonged to a thin woman with a dark raincoat and a long ponytail.

"*Mom!*" he said urgently, but everyone was singing again, and she didn't turn her head. The woman who had taken the wallet began to slip through the crowd. Instinctively, Brian began to follow her, afraid to lose sight of her. He turned back to call out to his mother again, but she was singing along now, too, "*God rest you merry, gentlemen . . .*" Everyone was singing so loud he knew she couldn't hear him.

For an instant, Brian hesitated as he glanced over his shoulder at his mother. Should he run back and get her? But he thought again about the medal that would make his father better; it was in the wallet, and he couldn't let it get stolen.

The woman was already turning the corner. He raced to catch up with her.

Why did I pick it up? Cally thought frantically as she rushed east on Forty-eighth Street toward Madison Avenue. She had abandoned her plan of walking down Fifth Avenue to find the peddler with the dolls. Instead, she headed toward the Lexington Avenue subway. She knew it would be quicker to go up to Fifty-first Street for the train, but the wallet felt like a hot brick in her pocket, and it seemed to her that everywhere she turned everyone was looking at her accusingly. Grand Central Station would be mobbed. She would get the train there. It was a safer place to go.

A squad car passed her as she turned right and crossed the street. Despite the cold, she had begun to perspire.

It probably belonged to that woman with the little boys. It was on the ground next to her. In her mind, Cally replayed the moment when she had taken in the slim young woman in the rose-colored all-weather coat that she could see was fur-lined from the turned-back sleeves. The coat obviously was expensive, as were the woman's shoulder bag and boots; the dark hair that came to the collar of her coat was shiny. She didn't look like she could have a care in the world.

Cally had thought, I wish I looked like that. She's about my age and my size and we have almost the same color hair. Well, maybe by next year I can afford pretty clothes for Gigi and me.

Then she'd turned her head to catch a glimpse of the Saks windows. So I didn't see her drop the wallet, she thought. But as she passed the woman, she'd felt her foot kick something and she'd looked down and seen it lying there.

Why didn't I just ask if it was hers? Cally agonized. But in that instant, she'd remembered how years ago, Grandma had come home one day, embarrassed and upset. She'd found a wallet on the street and opened it and saw the name and address of the owner. She'd walked three blocks to return it even though by then her arthritis was so bad that every step hurt.

The woman who owned it had looked through it and said that a twenty-dollar bill was missing.

Grandma had been so upset. "She practically accused me of being a thief."

That memory had flooded Cally the minute she touched the wallet. Suppose it did belong to the lady in the rose coat and she thought Cally had picked her pocket or taken money out of it? Suppose a policeman was called? They'd find out she was on probation. They wouldn't believe her any more than they'd believed her when she lent Jimmy money and her car because he'd told her if he didn't get out of town right away, a guy in another street gang was going to kill him.

Oh God, why didn't I just leave the wallet there? she thought. She considered tossing it in the nearest mailbox. She couldn't risk that. There were too many undercover cops around midtown during the holidays. Suppose one of them saw her and asked what she was doing? No, she'd get home right away. Aika, who minded Gigi along with her own grandchildren after the day-care center closed, would be bringing her home. It was getting late.

I'll put the wallet in an envelope addressed to whoever's name is in it and drop in in the mailbox later, Cally decided. That's all I can do.

Cally reached Grand Central Station. As she had hoped, it was mobbed with people rushing in all directions to trains and subways, hurrying home for Christmas. She shouldered her way across the main terminal, finally making it down the steps to the entrance to the Lexington Avenue subway.

As she dropped a token in the slot and hurried for the express train to Fourteenth Street, she was unaware of the small boy who had slipped under a turnstile and was dogging her footsteps.

2

"God rest you merry, gentlemen, let nothing you dismay . . ." The familiar words seemed to taunt Catherine, reminding her of the forces that threatened the happily complacent life she had assumed would be hers forever. Her husband was in the hospital with leukemia. His enlarged spleen had been removed this morning as a precaution against it rupturing, and while it was too early to tell for sure, he seemed to be doing well. Still, she could not escape the fear that he was not going to live, and the thought of life without him was almost paralyzing.

Why didn't I realize Tom was getting sick? she agonized. She remembered how only two weeks ago, when she'd asked him to take groceries from the car, he'd reached into the trunk for the heaviest bag, hesitated, then winced as he picked it up.

She'd laughed at him. "Play golf yesterday. Act like an old man today. Some athlete."

"Where's Brian?" Michael asked as he returned from dropping the dollar in the singer's basket.

Startled from her thoughts, Catherine looked down at her son. "Brian?" she said blankly. "He's right here." She glanced down at her side, and then her eyes scanned the area. "He had a dollar. Didn't he go with you to give it to the singer?"

"No," Michael said gruffly. "He probably kept it instead. He's a dork."

"Stop it," Catherine said. She looked around, suddenly alarmed. "Brian," she called "Brian." The carol was over, the crowd dispersing. Where was Brian? He wouldn't just walk away, surely *"Brian,"* she called out again, this time loudly, alarm clear in her voice.

A few people turned and looked at her curiously. "A little boy," she said, becoming frightened. "He's wearing a dark blue ski jacket and a red cap. Did anyone see where he went?"

She watched as heads shook, as eyes looked around, wanting to help. A woman pointed behind them to the lines of people waiting to see the Saks windows. "Maybe he went there?" she said in a heavy accent.

"How about the tree? Would he have crossed the street to get up close to it?" another woman suggested.

"Maybe the cathedral," someone volunteered.

"No. No, Brian wouldn't do that. We're going to visit his father. Brian can't wait to see him." As she said the words, Catherine knew that something was terribly wrong. She felt the tears that now came so easily rising behind her eyes. She fumbled in her bag for a handkerchief and realized something was missing: the familiar bulk of her wallet.

"Oh my God," she said. "My wallet's gone."

"Mom!" And now Michael lost the surly look that had

become his way of disguising the worry about his father. He was suddenly a scared ten-year-old. "Mom. Do you think Brian was kidnapped?"

"How could he be? Nobody could just drag him off. That's impossible." Catherine felt her legs were turning to rubber. "Call the police," she cried. "My little boy is missing."

The station was crowded. Hundreds of people were rushing in every direction. There were Christmas decorations all over the place. It was noisy, too. Sound of all kinds echoed through the big space, bouncing off the ceiling high above him. A man with his arm full of packages bumped a sharp elbow into Brian's ear. "Sorry, kid."

He was having trouble keeping up with the woman who had his mom's wallet. He kept losing sight of her. He struggled to get around a family with a couple of kids who were blocking his way. He got past them, but bumped into a lady who glared down at him. "Be careful," she snapped.

"I'm sorry," Brian said politely, looking up at her. In that second he almost lost the woman he was following, catching up to her again as she went down a staircase and hurried through a long corridor that led to a subway station. When she went through a turnstile, he slipped under the next one and followed her onto a train.

The car was so crowded he could hardly get in. The woman was standing, hanging onto a bar that ran over the seats along the side. Brian stood near her, his hand gripping a pole. They went only one long stop, then she pushed her way to the opening doors. So many people were in Brian's way that he almost didn't get out of the subway car in time, and then he had to hurry to catch up with her. He chased after her as she went up the stairs to another train.

This time the car wasn't as crowded, and Brian stood near an old lady who reminded him of his grandmother. The woman in the dark raincoat got off at the second stop and he followed her, his eyes fixed on her ponytail as she practically ran up the stairs to the street.

They emerged on a busy corner. Buses raced past in both directions, rushing to get across the wide street before the light turned red. Brian glanced behind him. As far as he could see down the block there were nothing but apartment houses. Light streamed from hundreds of windows.

The lady with the wallet stood waiting for the light to turn. The WALK sign flashed on, and he followed his quarry across the street. When she reached the other side she turned left and walked quickly down the now sloping sidewalk. As he followed her, Brian took a quick look at the street sign. When they visited last summer, his mother had made a game of teaching him about street signs in New York. "Gran lives on Eighty-seventh Street," she had said. "We're on Fiftieth. How many blocks away is her apartment?" This sign said Fourteenth Street. He had to remember that, he told himself, as he fell in step behind the woman with his mom's wallet.

He felt snowflakes on his face. It was getting windy, and the cold stung his cheeks. He wished a cop would come along so he could ask for help, but he didn't see one anywhere. He knew what he was going to do anyway—he would follow the lady to where she lived. He still had the dollar his mother had given him for the man who was playing the violin. He would get change and call his grandmother, and she'd send a cop who would get his mom's wallet back.

It's a good plan, he thought to himself. In fact, he was *sure* of it. He had to get the wallet, and the medal that was inside. He thought of how after Mom had said that the medal wouldn't do any good, Gran had put it in her hand and said, *Please give it to Tom and have faith.*

The look on his grandmother's face had been so calm and so sure that Brian knew she was right. Once he got the medal back and they gave it to his dad, he would get well. Brian *knew* it.

The woman with the ponytail started to walk faster. He chased after her as she crossed one street and went to the end of another block. Then she turned right.

The street they were on now wasn't bright with decorated store windows like the one they had just left. Some places were boarded up and there was a lot of writing on the buildings and some of the streetlights were broken. A guy with a beard was sitting on the curb, clutching a bottle. He stretched out his hand to Brian as he passed him.

For the first time, Brian felt scared, but he kept his eyes on the woman. The snow was falling faster now, and the sidewalk was getting slippery. He stumbled once, but managed not to fall. He was out of breath trying to keep up with the lady. How far was she going? he wondered. Four blocks later he had his answer. She stepped into the entranceway to an old building, stuck her key in the lock, and went inside. Brian raced to catch the door before it closed behind her, but he was too late. The door was locked.

Brian didn't know what to do next, but then through the glass he saw a man coming toward him. As the man opened the door and hurried past him, Brian managed to grab it and to duck inside before it closed again.

The hall was dark and dirty, and the smell of stale food hung in the air. Ahead of him he could hear footsteps going up the stairs. Gulping to swallow his fear, and trying to not make noise, Brian slowly began to climb to the first landing. He would see where the lady went; then he would get out of there and find a telephone. Maybe instead of calling Gran, he would dial 911, he thought.

His mom had taught him that that was what he should do when he *really* needed help.

Which so far he didn't.

"All right, Mrs. Dornan. Describe your son to me," the police officer said soothingly.

"He's seven and small for his age," Catherine said. She could hear the shrillness in her voice. They were sitting in a squad car, parked in front of Saks, near the spot where the violinist had been playing.

She felt Michael's hand clutch hers reassuringly.

"What color hair?" the officer asked.

Michael answered, "Like mine. Kind of reddish. His eyes are blue. He's got freckles and one of his front teeth is missing. He has the same kind of pants I'm wearing, and his jacket is like mine 'cept it's blue and mine is green. He's skinny."

The policeman looked approvingly at Michael. "You're a real help, son. Now, ma'am, you say your wallet is missing? Do you think you might have dropped it, or did anyone brush against you? I mean, could it have been a pickpocket?"

"I don't know," Catherine said. "I don't care about the

wallet. But when I gave the boys money for the violinist, I probably didn't push it down far enough in my purse. It was quite bulky and might have just fallen out."

"Your son wouldn't have picked it up and decided to go shopping?"

"No, no, no," Catherine said with a flash of anger, shaking her head emphatically. "Please don't waste time even considering that."

"Where do you live, ma'am? What I mean is, do you want to call anyone?" The policeman looked at the rings on Catherine's left hand. "Your husband?"

"My husband is in Sloan-Kettering hospital. He's very ill. He'll be wondering where we are. In fact, we should be with him soon. He's expecting us." Catherine put her hand on the door of the squad car. "I can't just sit here. I've got to look for Brian."

"Mrs. Dornan, I'm going to get Brian's description out right now. In three minutes every cop in Manhattan is going to be on the lookout for him. You know, he may have just wandered away and gotten confused. It happens. Do you come downtown often?"

"We used to live in New York, but we live in Nebraska now," Michael told him. "We visit my grandmother every summer. She lives on Eighty-seventh Street. We came back last week because my dad has leukemia and he needed an operation. He went to medical school with the doctor who operated on him."

Manuel Ortiz had been a policeman only a year, but already he had come in contact with grief and despair many times. He saw both in the eyes of this young woman. She had a husband who was very sick, now a missing kid. It was obvious to him that she could easily go into shock.

"Dad's gonna know something's wrong," Michael said, worried. "Mom, shouldn't you go see him?"

"Mrs. Dornan, how about leaving Michael with us? We'll stay here in case Brian tries to make his way back. We'll have all our guys looking for him. We'll fan out and use bullhorns to get him to contact us in case he's wandering around in the neighborhood somewhere. I'll get another car to take you up to the hospital and wait for you."

"You'll stay right here in case he comes back?"

"Absolutely."

"Michael, will you keep your eyes peeled for Brian?"

"Sure, Mom. I'll watch out for the Dork."

"Don't call him. . . ." Then Catherine saw the look on her son's face. He's trying to get a rise out of me, she thought. He's trying to convince me that Brian is fine. That he'll be fine.

She put her arms around Michael and felt his small, gruff embrace in return.

"Hang in there, Mom," he said.

3

Jimmy Siddons cursed silently as he walked through the oval near Avenue B in the Stuyvesant Town apartment complex. The uniform he had stripped from the prison guard gave him a respectable look but was much too dangerous to wear on the street. He'd managed to lift a filthy overcoat and knit cap from a homeless guy's shopping cart. They helped some, but he had to find something else to wear, something decent.

He also needed a car. He needed one that wouldn't be missed until morning, something parked for the night, the kind of car that one of these middle-class Stuyvesant Town residents would own: medium-sized, brown or black, looking like every other Honda or Toyota or Ford on the road. Nothing fancy.

So far he hadn't seen the right one. He had watched as some old geezer got out of a Honda and said to his passenger, "Sure's good to get home," but he was driving one of those shiny red jobs that screamed for attention.

A kid pulled up in an old heap and parked, but from the

sound of the engine, Jimmy wanted no part of it. Just what he'd need, he thought; get on the Thruway and have it break down.

He was cold and getting hungry. Ten hours in the car, he told himself. Then I'll be in Canada and Paige will meet me there and we'll disappear again. She was the first real girl-friend he'd ever had, and she'd been a big help to him in Detroit. He knew he never would have been caught last sum-mer if he had cased that gas station in Michigan better. He should have known enough to check the john outside the office instead of letting himself be surprised by an off-duty cop who stepped out of it while he was holding a gun on the attendant.

The next day he was on his way back to New York. To face trial for killing a cop.

An older couple passed him and threw a smile in his direc-tion. "Merry Christmas."

Jimmy responded with a courteous nod of the head. Then he paid close attention as he heard the woman say, "Ed, I can't believe you didn't put the presents for the children in the trunk. Who leaves anything in sight in a car overnight in this day and age?"

Jimmy went around the corner and then stepped into the deep shadows on the grass as he returned to watch the couple stop in front of a dark-colored Toyota. The man opened the door. From the backseat he took a small rocking horse and handed it to the woman, then scooped up a half-dozen brightly wrapped packages. With her help he transferred ev-erything to the trunk, relocked the car, and got back on the sidewalk.

Jimmy listened as the woman said, "I guess the phone's all

right in the glove compartment," and her husband answered, "Sure it is. Waste of money, as far as I'm concerned. Can't wait to see Bobby's face tomorrow when he opens everything."

He watched as they turned the corner and disappeared. Which meant from their apartment they wouldn't be able to glance out and notice an empty parking space.

Jimmy waited ten minutes before he walked to the car. A few snowflakes swirled around him. Two minutes later he was driving out of the complex. It was quarter after five. He was headed to Cally's apartment on Tenth and B. He knew she'd be surprised to see him. And none too happy. She probably thought he couldn't find her. Why did she suppose that he didn't have a way to keep track of her even from Riker's Island? he wondered.

Big sister, he thought, as he drove onto Fourteenth Street, you promised Grandma you'd take care of me! "Jimmy needs guidance," Grandma had said. "He's in with a bad crowd. He's too easily led." Well, Cally hadn't come to see him *once* in Riker's. Not once. He hadn't even heard from her.

He'd have to be careful. He was sure the cops would be watching for him around Cally's building. But he had that figured out, too. He used to hang around this neighborhood and knew how to get across the roofs from the other end of the block and into the building. A couple of times he'd even pulled a job there when he was a kid.

Knowing Cally, he was sure she still kept some of Frank's clothes in the closet. She'd been crazy about him, probably still had pictures of him all over the place. You'd never think he'd died even before Gigi was born.

And knowing Cally, she'd have at least a few bucks to get

her little brother through the tolls, he figured. He'd find a way to convince her to keep her mouth shut until he was safely in Canada with Paige.

Paige. An image of her floated through his mind. Luscious. Blond. Only twenty-two. Crazy about him. She'd arranged everything, gotten the gun smuggled in to him. She'd never let him down or turn her back on him.

Jimmy's smile was unpleasant. You never tried to help me while I was rotting in Riker's Island, he thought—but once again, sister dear, you're going to help me get away, like it or not.

He parked the car a block from the rear of Cally's building and pretended to be checking a tire as he looked around. No cops in sight. Even if they were watching Cally's place, they probably didn't know you could get to it through the boarded-up dump. As he straightened up he cursed. Damn bumper sticker. Too noticeable. WE'RE SPENDING OUR GRANDCHILDREN'S INHERITANCE. He managed to pull most of it off.

Fifteen minutes later, Jimmy had picked the flimsy lock of Cally's apartment and was inside. Some dump, he thought, as he took in the cracks in the ceiling and the worn linoleum in the tiny entranceway. But neat. Cally was always neat. A Christmas tree in the corner of what passed for a living room had a couple of small, brightly wrapped packages under it.

Jimmy shrugged and went into the bedroom, where he ransacked the closet to find the clothes he knew would be there. After changing, he went through the place looking for money but found none. He yanked open the doors that separated the stove, refrigerator, and sink from the living room, searched unsuccessfully for a beer, settled for a Pepsi, and made himself a sandwich.

From what his sources had told him, Cally should be home by now from her job in the hospital. He knew that on the way she picked up Gigi from the baby-sitter. He sat on the couch, his eyes riveted on the front door, his nerves jangling. He'd spent most of the few dollars he found in the guard's pockets on food from street vendors. He had to have money for the tolls on the Thruway, as well as enough for another tank of gas. Come on, Cally, he thought, where the hell are you?

At ten to six, he heard the key inserted in the lock. He jumped up and in three long strides was in the entryway, flattened against the wall. He waited until Cally stepped in and closed the door behind her, then put his hand over her mouth.

"Don't scream!" he whispered, as he muffled her terrified moan with his palm. "Understand?"

She nodded, eyes wide open in fear.

"Where's Gigi? Why isn't she with you?"

He released his grip long enough to let her gasp in an almost inaudible voice, "She's at the baby-sitter's. She's keeping her longer today, so I can shop. Jimmy, what are you *doing* here?"

"How much money have you got?"

"Here, take my pocketbook." Cally held it out to him, praying that he would not think to look through her coat pockets. Oh God, she thought, make him go away.

He took the purse and in a low and menacing tone warned, "Cally, I'm going to let go of you. Don't try anything or Gigi won't have a mommy waiting for her. Understand that?"

"Yes. Yes."

Cally waited until he released his grip on her, then slowly turned to face him. She hadn't seen her brother since that terrible night nearly three years ago when, with Gigi in her arms, she had come home from her job at the day-care center to find him waiting in her apartment in the West Village.

He looks about the same, she thought, except that his hair is shorter and his face is thinner. In his eyes there wasn't even a trace of the occasional warmth that at one time made her hope there was a possibility he might someday straighten out. No more. There was nothing left of the frightened six-year-old who had clung to her when their mother dumped them with Grandma and disappeared from their lives.

He opened her purse, rummaged through it, and pulled out her bright green combination change purse and billfold. "Eighteen dollars," he said angrily after a quick count of her money. "Is that all?"

"Jimmy, I get paid the day after tomorrow," Cally pleaded. "Please just take it and get out of here. Please leave me alone."

There's half a tank of gas in the car, Jimmy thought. There's money here for another half tank and the tolls. I might just be able to make Canada. He'd have to shut Cally up, of course, which should be easy enough. He would just warn her that if she put the cops onto him and he got caught, he'd swear that she got someone to smuggle the gun in to him that he'd used on the guard.

Suddenly a sound from outside made him whirl around. He put his eye to the peephole in the door but could see no one there. With a menacing gesture to Cally, indicating that she had better keep quiet, he noiselessly turned the knob and opened the door a fraction, just in time to see a small boy straighten up, turn, and start to tiptoe to the staircase.

In one quick movement, Jimmy flung open the door and scooped up the child, one arm around his waist, the other covering his mouth, and pulled him inside, then roughly set him down.

"Eavesdropping, kid? Who is this, Cally?"

"Jimmy, leave him alone. I don't know who he is," she cried. "I've never seen him before."

Brian was so scared he could hardly talk. But he could tell the man and woman were mad at each other. Maybe the man would help him get his mother's wallet back, he thought. He pointed to Cally. "She has my mom's wallet."

Jimmy released Brian. "Well, now *that's* good news," he said with a grin, turning to his sister. "Isn't it?"

4

A plainclothesman in an unmarked car drove Catherine to the hospital. "I'll wait right here, Mrs. Dornan," he said. "I have the radio on so we'll know the minute they find Brian."

Catherine nodded. *If they find Brian* raced through her mind. She felt her throat close against the terror that thought evoked.

The lobby of the hospital was decorated for the holiday season. A Christmas tree was in the center, garlands of evergreens were hung, and poinsettias were banked against the reception desk.

She got a visitor's pass and learned that Tom was now in room 530. She walked to the bank of elevators and entered a car already half full, mostly with hospital personnel—doctors in white jackets with the telltale pen and notebook in their breast pockets, attendants in green scrub suits, a couple of nurses.

Two weeks ago, Catherine thought, Tom was making his rounds at St. Mary's in Omaha, and I was Christmas shopping. That evening we took the kids out for hamburgers. Life was normal and good and fun, and we were joking about how last year Tom had had so much trouble getting the Christmas tree in the stand, and I promised him I'd buy a new stand before this Christmas Eve. And once again I thought Tom looked so tired, and I did nothing about it.

Three days later he collapsed.

"Didn't you push the fifth floor?" someone asked.

Catherine blinked. "Oh, yes, thank you." She got off the elevator and for a moment stood still, getting her bearings. She found what she was looking for, an arrow on the wall pointing toward rooms 515 to 530.

As she approached the nurses' station, she saw Spence Crowley. Her mouth went dry. Immediately following the operation this morning, he had assured her that it had gone smoothly, and that his assistant would be making the rounds this afternoon. Then why was Spence here now? she worried. Could something be wrong?

He spotted her and smiled. Oh God, he wouldn't smile if Tom were . . . It was another thought she could not finish.

He walked quickly around the desk and came to her. "Catherine, if you could *see* the look on your face! Tom's doing fine. He's pretty groggy, of course, but the vital signs are good."

Catherine looked up at him, wanting to believe the words she heard, wanting to trust the sincerity she saw in the brown eyes behind rimless glasses.

Firmly he took her arm and ushered her into the cubicle behind the nurses' station. "Catherine, I don't want to bully you, but you have to understand that Tom has a good chance of beating this thing. A very good chance. I have patients who've led useful, full lives with leukemia. There are different types of medicine to control it. The one I plan to use with Tom is Interferon. It's worked miracles with some of my patients. It will mean daily injections at first, but after we get the dosage adjusted, he'll be able to give them to himself. When he recuperates fully from the operation, he can go back to work, and I swear to you that's going to happen." Then he added quietly, "But there is a problem."

Now he looked stern. "This afternoon when you saw Tom in ICU, I understand you were pretty upset."

"Yes." She had tried not to cry but couldn't stop. She'd been so worried, and knowing that he had made it through the operation was such a relief that she couldn't help herself.

"Catherine, Tom just asked me to level with him. He thinks I told you it was hopeless. He's starting to not trust me. He's beginning to wonder if maybe I'm hiding something, that maybe things are worse than I'm telling him. Well, Catherine, that is simply not so, and your job is to convince him that you have every expectation that you two will have a long life together. He mustn't get it in his head that he has a very limited time, not only because that would be harmful to him, but equally important because I don't believe that's *true*. In order to get well, Tom needs faith in his chances to get better, and a great deal of that has to come from you."

"Spence, I should have *seen* he was getting sick." Spence put his arms around her shoulders in a brief hug. "Listen," he said, "there's an old adage, 'Physician, heal thyself.' When Tom is feeling better, I'm going to rake him over the coals for ignoring some of the warnings his body was giving him. But now, go in there with a light step and a happy face. You can do it."

Catherine forced a smile. "Like this?"

"Much better," he nodded. "Just keep smiling. Remember, it's Christmas. Thought you were bringing the kids tonight?"

She could not talk about Brian being missing. Not now. Instead, she practiced what she would tell Tom. "Brian was sneezing, and I want to make sure he's not starting with a cold."

"That was wise. Okay. See you tomorrow, kiddo. Now remember, keep that smile going. You're gorgeous when you smile."

Catherine nodded and started down the hall to room 530. She opened the door quietly. Tom was asleep. An IV unit was dripping fluid into his arm. Oxygen tubes were in his nostrils. His skin was as white as the pillowcase. His lips were ashen.

The private duty nurse stood up. "He's been asking for you, Mrs. Dornan. I'll wait outside."

Catherine pulled up a chair next to the bed. She sat down and placed her hand over the one lying on the coverlet. She studied her husband's face, scrutinizing every detail: the high forehead framed by the reddish brown hair that was exactly the color of Brian's; the thick eyebrows that always looked a bit unruly; the well-shaped nose and the lips that were usually parted in a smile. She thought of his eyes, more blue than gray, and the warmth and understanding they conveyed. He gives confidence to his patients, she thought. Oh, Tom, I want to tell you that our little boy is missing. I want you to be well and with me, looking for him.

Tom Dornan opened his eyes. "Hi, Love," he said weakly.

"Hi, yourself." She bent over and kissed him. "I'm sorry I

was such a wimp this afternoon. Call it PMS or just old-fashioned relief. You know what a sentimental slob I am. I even cry at happy endings."

She straightened up and looked directly into his eyes. "You're doing great. You really are, you know."

She could see he did not believe her. *Not yet*, she thought determinedly.

"I thought you were bringing the kids tonight?" His voice was low and halting.

She realized that with Tom it was not possible to utter Brian's name without breaking down. Instead she said quickly, "I was afraid they'd be hanging all over you. I thought it was a good idea to let them wait until tomorrow morning."

"Your mother phoned," Tom said drowsily. "The nurse spoke to her. She said she sent a special present for you to give me. What is it?"

"Not without the boys. They want to be the ones to give it to you."

"Okay. But be sure to bring them in the morning. I want to see them."

"For sure. But since it's just the two of us now, maybe I should climb in the sack with you."

Tom opened his eyes again. "Now you're talking." A smile flickered on his lips. And then he was asleep again.

For a long moment, she laid her head on the bed, then got up as the nurse tiptoed back in. "Doesn't he look fantastic?" Catherine asked brightly as the nurse put her fingers on Tom's pulse.

She knew that even slipping into sleep, Tom might hear

her. Then with a last glance at her husband, she hurried from the room, down the corridor and to the elevator, then through the lobby, and into the waiting police car.

The plainclothesman answered her unasked question: "No word so far, Mrs. Dornan."

5

"I said, give it to me," Jimmy Siddons said ominously.

Cally tried to brave it out. "I don't know what this boy is talking about, Jimmy."

"Yes, you do," Brian said. "I saw you pick up my mom's wallet. And I followed you because I have to get it back."

"Aren't you a smart kid?" Siddons sneered. "Always go where the buck is." His expression turned ugly as he faced his sister. "Don't make me take it from you, Cally."

There was no use trying to pretend she didn't have it. Jimmy knew the boy was telling the truth. Cally still had her coat on. She reached into the pocket and took out the handsome Moroccan leather wallet. Silently she handed it to her brother.

"That belongs to my mother," Brian said defiantly. Then the glance the man gave him made him shiver. He had been about to try to grab the wallet; instead, now suddenly fearful, he dug his hands deep in his pockets.

Jimmy Siddons opened the billfold. "My, my," he said, his

tone now admiring. "Cally, you surprise me. You run rings around some of the pickpockets I know."

"I didn't steal it," Cally protested. "Someone dropped it, I found it. I was going to mail it back."

"Well, you can forget that," Jimmy said. "It's mine now, and I need it."

He pulled out a thick wad of bills and began counting. "Three hundred-dollar bills, four fifties, six twenties, four tens, five fives, three ones. Six hundred and eighty-eight dollars. Not bad, in fact, it'll do just fine."

He stuffed the money in the pocket of the suede jacket he had taken from the bedroom closet and began to dig through the compartments in the wallet. "Credit cards. Well, why not? Driver's license—no, two of them: Catherine Dornan and Dr. Thomas Dornan. Who's Dr. Thomas Dornan, kid?"

"My dad. He's in the hospital." Brian watched as the deep compartment in the wallet revealed the medal.

Jimmy Siddons lifted it out, held it up by the chain, then laughed incredulously. "St. Christopher! I haven't been inside a church in years, but even I know they kicked him out long ago. And when I think of all the stories Grandma used to tell us about how he carried the Christ child on his shoulders across the stream or the river or whatever it was! Remember, Cally?" Disdainfully he let the medal clatter to the floor.

Brian swooped to retrieve it. He clutched it in his hand, then slipped it around his neck. "My grandpa carried it all through the war and came home safe. It's going to make my dad get better. I don't care about the wallet. You can have it. This is what I really wanted. I'm going home now." He turned and ran for the door. He had twisted the knob and pulled the door open before Siddons reached him, clapped a hand over his mouth, and yanked him back inside.

"You and St. Christopher are staying right here with me, buddy," he said as he shoved him roughly to the floor.

Brian gasped as his forehead slammed onto the cracked linoleum. He sat up slowly, rubbing his head. He felt like the room was spinning, but he could hear the woman he had followed pleading with the man. "Jimmy, don't hurt him. Please. Leave us alone. Take the money and go. But get out of here."

Brian wrapped his arms around his legs, trying not to cry. He shouldn't have followed the lady. He knew that now. He should have yelled instead of following her so that maybe somebody would stop her. This man was bad. This man wasn't going to let him go home. And nobody knew where he was. Nobody knew where to look for him.

He felt the medal dangling against his chest and closed his fist around it. Please get me back to Mom, he prayed silently, so I can bring you to Dad.

He did not look up to see Jimmy Siddons studying him. He did not know that Jimmy's mind was racing, assessing the situation. This kid followed Cally when she took the wallet, Siddons thought. Did anyone follow him? No. If they had, they'd be here by now. "Where did you get the wallet?" he asked his sister.

"On Fifth Avenue. Across from Rockefeller Center." Cally was terrified now. Jimmy would stop at nothing to get away. Not at killing her. Not at killing this child. "His mother must have dropped it. I picked it up off the sidewalk. I guess he saw me."

"I guess he did." Jimmy looked at the phone on the table next to the couch. Then, grinning, he reached for the cellular phone he had taken from the glove compartment of the stolen car. He also took out a gun and pointed it at Cally. "The cops may have your phone tapped." He pointed at the table next to the couch. "Go over there. I'm going to dial your number and tell you I'm turning myself in and I want you to call that public defender who is representing me. All you have to do is act nice and nervous, just like you are now. Make a mistake and you and this kid are dead."

He looked down at Brian. "One peep out of you and . . ." He left the threat unspoken.

Brian nodded to show he understood. He was too scared to even promise that he'd be quiet.

"Cally, you got all that straight?"

Cally nodded. How stupid I've been, she thought. I was fool enough to believe I'd gotten away from him. No chance. He even knows this phone number.

He finished dialing and the phone beside her rang. "Hello." Her voice was low and muffled.

"Cally, it's Jimmy. Listen, I'm in trouble. You probably know by now. I'm sorry I tried to get away. I hope that guard will be all right. I'm broke and I'm scared.". Jimmy's voice was a whine. "Call Gil Weinstein. He's the public defender assigned to me. Tell him I'll meet him at St. Patrick's Cathedral when midnight Mass is over. Tell him I want to turn myself in and I want him to be with me. His home number is 555-0267. Cally, I'm sorry I messed up everything so badly."

Jimmy pressed the disconnect on the cellular phone and watched as Cally hung up as well. "They can't trace a cellular phone call, you know that, don't you? Okay, now phone

Weinstein and give him the same story. If the cops are listening, they must be jumping up and down right now."

"Jimmy, they'll think I . . ."

In two steps Jimmy was beside her, the gun to her head. "Make the call."

"Your lawyer may not be home. He may refuse to meet you."

"Naw. I know him. He's a jerk. He'll want the publicity. Get him."

Cally did not need to be told to make it quick. The moment Gil Weinstein was on the line, she rushed to say, "You don't know me. I'm Cally Hunter. My brother, Jimmy Siddons, just called. He wants me to tell you . . ." In a quavering voice she delivered the message.

"I'll meet him," the lawyer said. "I'm glad he's doing this, but if that prison guard dies, Jimmy is facing a death-penalty trial. He could get life without parole for the first killing, but now . . ." His voice trailed off.

"I think he knows that." Cally saw Jimmy's gesture. "I have to go now. Good-bye, Mr. Weinstein."

"You make a great accomplice, big sister," Jimmy told her. He looked down at Brian. "What's your name, kid?"

"Brian," he whispered.

"Come on, Brian. We're getting out of here."

"Jimmy, leave him alone. Please. Leave him here with me."

"No way. There's always the chance you'd go running to the cops even though the minute they talk to that kid, you're in big trouble yourself. After all, you *did* steal his mama's wallet. No, the kid comes with me. No one is looking for a guy with his little boy, are they? I'll let him go tomorrow morning when I get to where I'm headed. After that you can tell them anything you like about me. The kid'll even back you up, won't you, sonny?"

Brian shrank against Cally. He was so afraid of the man that he was trembling. Was the man going to make him go away with him?

"Jimmy, leave him here. Please." Cally thrust Brian behind her.

Jimmy Siddons's mouth twisted in anger. He grabbed Cally's arm and yanked her toward him, roughly twisting her arm behind her.

She screamed as she lost her grip on Brian and slipped to the floor.

With eyes that denied any history of affection between them, Jimmy stood over his sister, again holding the gun to her head. "If you don't do what I tell you, you'll get more of that . . . and worse. They won't take me alive. Not you, not nobody else is gonna send me to the death chamber. Besides, I got a girlfriend waiting for me. So just keep your mouth shut. I'll even make a deal. You don't say nothing, and I'll let the kid live. But if the cops try to close in on me, he gets a bullet in the head. It's as simple as that. Got it straight?"

He stuck the gun back inside his jacket, then reached down and roughly pulled Brian to his feet. "You and I are gonna get to be real pals, sonny," he said. "Real pals." He grinned. "Merry Christmas, Cally."

6

The unmarked van parked across the street from Cally's apartment building was the lookout post for the detectives watching Cally's building for any sign of Jimmy Siddons. They had observed Cally come home at just a little after her usual time.

Jack Shore, the detective who had visited Cally in the morning, pulled off his earphones, swore silently, and turned to his partner. "What do you think, Mort? No, wait a minute. I'll tell you what I think. It's a trick. He's trying to buy time to get as far away from New York as possible while we take up the collection at St. Pat's looking for him."

Mort Levy, twenty years younger than Shore and less cynical, rubbed his chin, always a sign that he was deep in thought. "If it is a trick, I don't think the sister is a willing accomplice. You don't need a meter to hear the stress level in her voice."

"Listen, Mort, you were at Bill Grasso's funeral. Thirty years old, with four little kids, and shot between the eyes by that bum Siddons. If Cally Hunter had come clean with us and told us that she'd given that rat brother of hers money and the keys to her car, Grasso would have known what he was up against when he stopped him for running a light."

"I still believe that Cally had bought Jimmy's story about trying to get away because he'd been in a gang fight and the other gang was after him. I don't think she knew that he'd wounded a clerk in a liquor store. Up till then he hadn't been in really serious trouble."

"You mean he'd gotten away with it till then," Shore snapped. "Too bad that judge couldn't put Cally away as an accessory to murder instead of just for aiding a fugitive. She got off after serving fifteen months. Bill Grasso's widow is trimming the tree without him tonight."

His face reddened with anger. "I'll call in. Just in case that louse meant what he said, we've got to cover the cathedral. You know how many people go to midnight Mass there tonight? Take a guess."

Cally sat on the worn velour sofa, her hands clasped around her knees, her head bent, her eyes closed. Her entire body was trembling. She was beyond tears, beyond fatigue. Dear God, dear God, *why* did all this happen?

What should she do?

If anything happened to Brian, she would be responsible. She had picked up his mother's wallet, and that's why he'd followed her. If the child was right, his dad was very ill. She thought of the attractive young woman in the rose-colored coat and how she had been sure everything in her life was perfect.

Would Jimmy let the boy go when he got to wherever was his destination? How could he? she reasoned. Wherever that was, they'd start searching for Jimmy in that area. *And if he does let him go, Brian will tell how he followed me because I took the wallet,* she reminded herself.

But Jimmy had said he would shoot the child if the cops closed in on him. And he meant it, she was certain of that. So if I tell the cops, Brian doesn't have a chance, she thought.

If I don't say anything now and Jimmy does let him go, then I can honestly say that I didn't tell because he threatened to kill the kid if the cops got near him, and I knew he meant it. And I know he does mean it, Cally thought. That's the worst part.

Brian's face loomed in Cally's mind. The reddish brown hair that fell forward on his forehead, the large, intelligent blue eyes, the spatter of freckles on his cheeks and nose. When Jimmy dragged him in, her first impression was that he wasn't more than five; from the way he spoke, though, she was sure he was older. He was so scared when Jimmy made him go with him out the window and onto the fire escape. He had looked back at her, his eyes pleading.

The phone rang. It was Aika, the wonderful black woman who minded Gigi along with her own grandchildren each afternoon after the day-care center closed.

"Just checking to see if you're home, Cally," Aika said, her voice rich and comforting. "Did you find the doll man?"

"I'm afraid not."

"Too bad. You need more time to shop?"

"No, I'll come right over now and get Gigi."

"No, that's okay. She already ate dinner with my gang. I need milk for breakfast, so I've got to go out anyway. I'll drop her off in half an hour or so."

"Thanks, Aika." Cally put down the receiver, aware that

she still had her coat on and that the apartment was dark except for the entryway light. She took off the coat, went into the bedroom, and opened the closet door. She gasped when she saw that when he took Frank's suede jacket and brown slacks, Jimmy had left other clothes crumpled on the floor, a jacket and pants, and a filthy overcoat.

She bent down and picked up the jacket. Detective Shore had told her that Jimmy had shot a guard and stripped him of his uniform. Obviously, this was the uniform—and there were bullet holes in the jacket.

Frantically, Cally wrapped the jacket and pants inside the overcoat. Suppose the cops came in with a search warrant! They'd never believe her, that Jimmy broke into her place. They'd be sure she gave him clothes. She'd go back to prison. And she'd lose Gigi for good! What should she do?

She looked around the closet, wildly searching for a solution. The storage box on the overhead shelf. In it she kept whatever summer clothes she and Gigi had. She yanked the box down, opened it, pulled out the contents, and threw them on the shelf. She folded the uniform and coat into the box, closed it, ran to the bed, and fished under it for the Christmas wrappings she had stored there.

With frantic fingers she wrapped candy-cane paper around the box and tied it with a ribbon. Then she carried it into the living room and put it under the tree. She had just completed the task when she heard the downstairs buzzer. Smoothing back her hair, and forcing a welcoming smile for Gigi, she went to answer it.

It was Detective Shore and the other detective who had been with him this morning who came up the stairs. "Playing games again, Cally?" Shore asked. "I hope not."

7

Brian huddled in the passenger seat as Jimmy Siddons drove up the East River Drive. He had never felt so afraid before. He'd been scared when the man made him climb up that fire escape to the roof. Then he'd practically been dragged from one roof to another as they went the length of the block, finally going down through an empty building and onto the street where this car was parked.

The man had pushed Brian into the car and snapped on the seat belt. "Just remember to call me Daddy if anyone stops us," he had warned him.

Brian knew the man's name was Jimmy. That was what the woman had called him. She had looked so worried about Brian. When Jimmy pulled him through the window, she had been crying, and Brian could tell how scared she was for him. She knew his parents' names. Maybe she would call the cops. If she did, would they come looking for him? But Jimmy said he'd kill him if the cops came. Would he?

Brian huddled deeper in the seat. He was scared and hungry. And he had to go to the bathroom, but he was afraid to ask. His only comfort was the medal that now lay against his chest on the outside of his jacket. It had brought Grandpa home from the war. It was going to make Daddy well. And it was going to get him home safe, too. He was sure of it.

Jimmy Siddons glanced briefly at his small hostage. For the first time since he had broken out of the prison, he was beginning to relax. It was still snowing, but if it didn't get any worse than this, it was nothing to worry about. Cally wouldn't call the cops. He was positive of that. She knew him well enough to believe him when he said he would kill the kid if he was stopped.

I'm not going to rot in prison for the rest of my life, he thought, and I'm not giving them the chance to pump me full of poison. Either I make it, or I don't.

But I *will*. He smiled grimly. He knew there had to be an APB out on him and they'd be watching all the bridges and tunnels out of New York. But they had no idea where he was heading, and they certainly weren't looking for a father and son traveling in a car that wasn't reported stolen yet.

He'd pulled out all the presents he had seen the couple stash in the trunk. Now they were piled on the backseat, bundles of Christmas cheer. Those presents, coupled with the kid in the front, meant even if toll takers had been alerted to be on the lookout, they'd never glance twice at him now.

And in eight or nine hours he would be across the border and into Canada, where Paige would be waiting. And then he would find a nice deep lake that would be the final destination of this car and all the nice presents in the backseat.

And this kid with his St. Christopher medal.

* * *

The awesome power of the New York City Police Department ground methodically into gear as plans were laid to assure that Jimmy Siddons did not slip between their fingers, just in case, at the last minute, he panicked and decided not to surrender after midnight Mass.

As soon as their wiretap recorded Cally's phone calls from Jimmy, and to his lawyer, Jack Shore had called in the information. He had let the higher-ups know exactly what he thought of Siddons's "decision" to surrender. "It's an out-and-out crock," he had barked. "We tie up a couple of hundred cops till one-thirty or two in the morning, and he's halfway to Canada or Mexico before we find out that he's made us look like a bunch of fools."

Finally the deputy police commissioner in charge of the manhunt had snapped, "All right, Jack. We *know* what you think. Now let's get on with it. There's been no sign of him around his sister's place?"

"No, sir," Jack Shore had said and hung up, and then he and his partner, Mort, had gone to visit Cally. When they got back to the van, Shore again reported in to headquarters. "We just were back to Hunter's apartment, sir. She's fully aware of the consequences if she helps her brother in any way. The baby-sitter dropped off her kid as we were leaving, and my guess is Cally's in for the night."

Mort Levy frowned as he listened to his partner's conversation with the deputy police commissioner. There was something about that apartment that was *different* from the way it had looked this morning, but he couldn't figure out what it was. Mentally he reviewed the layout: the small entryway, the bathroom directly off it, the narrow combination living room—kitchen, the cell-like bedroom, barely large enough to hold a single bed, a cot for the little girl, and a three-drawer dresser.

Jack had asked Cally if she would mind if they looked around again, and she had nodded assent. Certainly no one was hiding in that place. They had opened the door to the bathroom, looked under the beds, poked in the closet. Levy had felt unwilling pity for Cally Hunter's attempts to brighten the dismal flat. All the walls were painted a bright yellow. Floral pillows were randomly piled on the old couch. The Christmas tree was bravely decorated with tons of tinsel and strings of red and green lights. A few brightly wrapped presents were placed under it.

Presents? Mort did not know why this word triggered something in his subconscious. He thought for a moment, then shook his head. Forget it, he told himself.

He wished Jack hadn't bullied Cally Hunter. It was easy to see that she was terrified of him. Mort hadn't been in on her case, which had been tried over two years ago, but from what he'd heard, he believed that Cally honestly thought that her troublesome kid brother had been in a gang fight and that the members of the other gang were hunting him.

What am I trying to remember about her apartment? Mort asked himself. *What was different?*

They were normally scheduled to go off duty at eight o'clock, but tonight both he and Jack were going back to headquarters instead. Like dozens of others, they would be working overtime at least until after midnight Mass at the cathedral. Maybe, just maybe, Siddons would show up as he had promised. Levy knew that Shore was aching to make the arrest personally. "I could spot that guy if he was wearing a nun's habit," he kept saying, over and over again.

There was a tap at the back door of the van, signifying that their replacements had arrived. As Mort stood up, stretched, and stepped down onto the street, he was glad that just before he left Cally Hunter's apartment, he had slipped her his card and whispered, "If you want to talk to anyone, Mrs. Hunter, here's a number where you can reach me."

8

The crowds on Fifth Avenue had thinned out, although there were still some onlookers around the tree in Rockefeller Center. Others were still lined up waiting to see Saks's window display, and there was a steady stream of visitors slipping in and out of St. Patrick's Cathedral.

But as the car she was in pulled up behind the squad car where Officer Ortiz and Michael were waiting, Catherine could see that most of the last-minute shoppers were gone.

They're on their way home, she thought, to do the final gift wrapping and to tell each other that next year, for sure, they won't be rushing around to stores on Christmas Eve.

Everything at the last minute. That had been her own pattern until twelve years ago, when a third-year resident, Dr. Thomas Dornan, came into the administration office of St. Vincent's Hospital, walked over to her desk, and said, "You're new here, aren't you?"

Tom, so easygoing, but so organized. If she were the one who was sick, Tom wouldn't have stuffed all her money and identification into his own bulging wallet. He wouldn't have dropped it into his pocket so carelessly that someone either reached in and grabbed it or picked it up off the ground.

That was the thought that was torturing Catherine as she opened the car door and, through the swirling snow, ran the few steps to the squad car. Brian would never have wandered away on his own, she was sure of that. He was so anxious to get to Tom, he hadn't even wanted to take the time to look at the Rockefeller Center tree. He must have set off on some mission. That was it. If somebody hadn't actually kidnapped him—and that seemed unlikely—he must have seen whoever took or picked up the wallet and followed that person.

Michael was sitting in the front seat with Officer Ortiz, sipping a soda. A brown paper bag with remnants of a packet of ketchup was standing on the floor in front of him. Catherine squeezed in beside him on the front seat and smoothed his hair.

"How's Dad?" he asked anxiously. "You didn't tell him about Brian, did you?"

"No, of course not. I'm sure we'll find Brian soon, and there was no need to worry him. And he's doing just great. I saw Dr. Crowley. He's a happy camper about Dad." She looked over Michael's head at Officer Ortiz. "It's been almost two hours," she said quietly.

He nodded. "Brian's description will keep going out every hour to every cop and car in the area. Mrs. Dornan, Michael and I have been talking. He's sure Brian wouldn't deliberately wander away."

"No, he's right. He wouldn't."

"You talked to the people around you when you realized he was missing?"

"Yes."

"And no one noticed a kid being pulled or carried away?"

"No. People remember seeing him, then they didn't see him."

"I'll level with you. I don't know any molester who would even attempt to kidnap a child from his mother's side and work his way through a crowd of people. But Michael thinks that maybe Brian would have taken off after someone he saw take your wallet."

Catherine nodded. "I've been thinking the same thing. It's the only answer that makes sense."

"Michael tells me that last year Brian stood up to a fourth-grade kid who shoved one of his classmates."

"He's a gutsy kid," Catherine said. Then the import of what the policeman had said hit her. *He thinks that if Brian followed whoever took my wallet, he may have confronted that person.* Oh God, no!

"Mrs. Dornan, if it's all right with you, I think it would be a good idea if we tried to get cooperation from the media. We might be able to get some of the local TV stations to show Brian's picture if you have one."

"The one I carried is in my wallet," Catherine said, her voice a monotone. Images of Brian standing up to a thief flashed in her mind. My little boy, she thought, would some-one hurt my little boy?

What was Michael saying? He was talking to the cop Ortiz.

"My grandmother has a bunch of pictures of us," Michael was telling him. Then he looked up at his mother. "Anyhow, Mom, you gotta call Gran. She's going to start worrying if we're not home soon."

Like father, like son, Catherine thought. Brian looks like

Tom. Michael thinks like him. She closed her eyes against the waves of near panic that washed through her. Tom. Brian. Why?

She felt Michael fishing in her shoulder bag. He pulled out the cellular phone. "I'll dial Gran," he told her.

9

In her apartment on Eighty-seventh Street, Barbara Cavanaugh clutched the phone, not wanting to believe what her daughter was telling her. But there was no disputing the dreadful news that Catherine's quiet, almost emotionless voice had conveyed. Brian was missing, and had been missing for over two hours now.

Barbara managed to keep her voice calm. "Where are you, dear?"

"Michael and I are in a police car at Forty-ninth and Fifth. That's where we were standing when Brian . . . just suddenly wasn't next to me."

"I'll be right there."

"Mom, be sure to bring the most recent pictures you have of Brian. The police want to give them out to all the news media. And the news radio station is going to have me on in a few minutes to make an appeal. And Mom, call the nurses' station on the fifth floor of the hospital. Tell them to make absolutely sure that Tom isn't allowed to turn on the TV in his room. He doesn't have a radio. If he ever found out that Brian was missing . . ." Her voice trailed off.

"I'll call right away but, Catherine, I don't have any recent pictures here," Barbara cried. "All the ones we took last summer are in the Nantucket house." Then she wanted to bite her lip. She'd been asking for new pictures of the boys and hadn't received any. Only yesterday Catherine had told her that her Christmas present, framed portraits of them, had been forgotten in the rush to get Tom to New York for the operation.

"I'll bring what I can find," she said hurriedly. "I'm on my way."

For an instant after she finished delivering the message to the hospital, Barbara Cavanaugh sank into a chair and rested her forehead in her palm. Too much, she thought, too much.

Had there always been a feeling haunting her that everything was too good to be true? Catherine's father had died when she was ten, and there had always been a lingering touch of sadness in her eyes, until at twenty-two she met Tom. They were so happy together, so perfect together. The way Gene and I were from day one, Barbara thought.

For an instant her mind rushed back to that moment in 1943, when at age nineteen and a sophomore in college, she'd been introduced to a handsome young Army officer, Lieutenant Eugene Cavanaugh. In that first moment they'd both known that they were perfect for each other. They were married two months later, but it was eighteen years before their only child was born.

With Tom, my daughter has found the same kind of relationship with which I was blessed, Barbara thought, but now

. . . She jumped up. She *had* to get to Catherine. Brian *must* have just wandered away. They just got separated, she told herself. Catherine was strong, but she must be close to the breaking point by now. Oh, dear God, let someone find him, she prayed.

She rushed through the apartment, yanking framed photographs from mantels and tabletops. She'd moved here from Beekman Place ten years ago. It was still more space than she needed, with a formal dining room, library, and guest suite. But now it meant that when Tom and Catherine and the boys came to visit from their home in Omaha, there was plenty of room for them.

Barbara tossed the pictures into the handsome leather carryall Tom and Catherine had given her for her birthday, grabbed a coat from the foyer closet, and, without bothering to double lock the door, rushed outside in time to press the button for the elevator as it began to descend from the penthouse.

Sam, the elevator operator, was a longtime employee. When he opened the door for her, his smile was replaced by a look of concern. "Good evening, Mrs. Cavanaugh. Merry Christmas. Any further word on Dr. Dornan?"

Afraid to speak, Barbara shook her head.

"Those grandkids of yours are real cute. The little one, Brian, told me you gave his mom something that would make his dad get well. I sure hope that's true."

Barbara tried to say, "So do I," but found that her lips could not form the words.

"Mommy, why are you sad?" Gigi asked as she settled onto Cally's lap.

"I'm not sad, Gigi," Cally said. "I'm always happy when I'm with you."

Gigi shook her head. She was wearing a red-and-white Christmas nightgown with figures of angels carrying candles. Her wide brown eyes and wavy golden-brown hair were legacies from Frank. The older she gets, the more she looks like him, Cally thought, instinctively holding the child tighter.

They were curled up together on the couch across from the Christmas tree. "I'm glad you're home with me, Mommy," Gigi said, and her voice became fearful. "You won't leave me again, will you?"

"No. I didn't want to leave you last time, sweetheart."

"I didn't like visiting you at that place."

That place. The Bedford correctional facility for women.

"I didn't like being there." Cally tried to sound matter-of-fact.

"Kids should stay with their mothers."

"Yes. I think so too."

"Mommy, is that big present for me?" Gigi pointed to the box that held the uniform and coat Jimmy had discarded.

Cally's lips went dry. "No, sweetheart, that's a present for Santa Claus. He likes to get something for Christmas, too. Now come on, it's past your bedtime."

Gigi automatically began to say, "I don't want to . . . ," then she stopped. "Will Christmas come faster if I go to bed now?"

"Uh-huh. Come on, I'll carry you in."

When she had tucked the blankets around Gigi and given her her "bee," the tattered blanket that was her daughter's indispensable sleeping companion, Cally went back to the living room and once again sank down onto the couch.

Kids should stay with their mothers . . . Gigi's words haunted her. Dear God, where had Jimmy taken that little boy? What would he do to him? What should she do?

Cally stared at the box with the candy-cane paper. *That's for Santa Claus.* A vivid memory of its contents flashed through her mind. The uniform of the guard Jimmy had shot, the side and sleeve still sticky with blood. The filthy overcoat —God knew where he'd found or stolen *that.*

Jimmy was *evil.* He had no conscience, no pity. Face it, Cally told herself fiercely—he won't hesitate to kill that little boy if it helps his chances to escape.

She turned on the radio to the local news. It was seven-thirty. The breaking news was that the condition of the prison guard who had been shot at Riker's Island was still critical, but was now stable. The doctors were cautiously optimistic that he would live.

If he lives, Jimmy isn't facing the death penalty, Cally told herself. They can't execute him now for the cop's death three years ago. He's smart. He won't take a chance on murdering the little boy once he knows that the guard isn't going to die. He'll let him go.

The announcer was saying, "In other news, early this evening, seven-year-old Brian Dornan became separated from his mother on Fifth Avenue. The family is in New York because Brian's father . . ."

Frozen in front of the radio, Cally listened as the announcer gave a description of the boy, then said, "Here is a plea from his mother, asking for your help."

As Cally listened to the low, urgent voice of Brian's mother, she visualized the young woman who had dropped the wallet. Early thirties at the most. Shiny, dark hair that just reached the collar of her coat. She'd only caught a glimpse of her face, but Cally was sure that she was very pretty. Pretty and well dressed and secure.

Now, listening to her begging for help, Cally put her hands over her ears, then ran to the radio and snapped it off. She tiptoed into the bedroom. Gigi was already asleep, her breathing soft and even, her cheek pillowed in her hand, the other hand holding the ragged baby blanket up to her face.

Cally knelt beside her. I can reach out and touch her, she thought. That woman can't reach out to her child. What should I do? But if I call the police and Jimmy does harm that little boy, they'll say it's my fault, just the way they said that the cop's death was my fault.

Maybe Jimmy will just leave him somewhere. He *promised* he would . . . Even Jimmy wouldn't hurt a little boy, surely? I'll just wait and pray, she told herself.

But the prayer she tried to whisper—"Please God, keep little Brian safe"—sounded like a mockery and she did not complete it.

Jimmy had decided that his best bet was to go over the George Washington Bridge to Route 4, then take Route 17 to the New York Thruway. It might be a little farther that way than going up through the Bronx to the Tappan Zee, but every instinct warned him to get out of New York City fast. It was good that the GW had no toll gate at the outgoing side where they might stop him.

Brian looked out the window as they crossed the bridge. He knew they were going over the Hudson River. His mother had cousins who lived in New Jersey, near the bridge. Last summer, when he and Michael spent an extra week with

Gran after they came back from Nantucket, they had visited them there.

They were nice. They had kids just about his age, too. Just thinking about them made Brian want to cry. He wished he could open the window and shout, *"I'm here. Come get me, please!"*

He was so hungry, and he really had to go to the bathroom. He looked up timidly. "I . . . could I please . . . I mean, I have to go to the bathroom." Now that he'd said it, he was so afraid the man would refuse that his lip began to quiver. Quickly he bit down on it. He could just hear Michael calling him a crybaby. But even that thought made him feel sad. He wouldn't even mind seeing Michael right now.

"You gotta pee?"

The man didn't seem too mad at him. Maybe he wouldn't hurt him after all. "Uh-huh."

"Okay. You hungry?"

"Yes, sir."

Jimmy was starting to feel somewhat secure. They were on Route 4. The traffic was heavy but moving. Nobody was looking for this car. By now, the guy who parked it was probably in his pj's watching *It's a Wonderful Life* for the fortieth time. By tomorrow morning, when he and his wife started to holler about their stolen Toyota, Jimmy would be in Canada with Paige. God he was crazy about her. In his life, she was the closest he had ever come to a sure thing.

Jimmy didn't want to stop to eat yet. On the other hand, to be on the safe side, he probably should fill up the tank now. There was no telling what hours places would keep on Christmas Eve.

"All right," he said, "in a couple minutes we'll get some

gas, go to the john, and I'll buy sodas and potato chips. Later on, we'll stop at a McDonald's and get a hamburger. But just remember when we stop for gas, you try to attract attention and . . ." He pulled the pistol from his jacket, pointed it at Brian, and made a clicking noise. *"Bang,"* he said.

Brian looked away. They were in the middle lane of the three-lane highway. A sign pointed to the exit marked Forest Avenue. A police car pulled abreast of them, then turned off into the parking lot of a diner. "I won't talk to anyone. I promise," he managed to say.

"I promise, *Daddy,"* Jimmy snapped.

Daddy. Involuntarily, Brian's hand curled around the St. Christopher medal. He was going to bring this medal to Daddy and then Daddy was going to get better. Then his dad would find this guy, Jimmy, and beat him up for being so mean to his kid. Brian was sure of it. As his fingers traced the raised image of the towering figure carrying the Christ child, he said in a clear voice, "I promise, *Daddy."*

10

At lower Manhattan's One Police Plaza, the command post for the Jimmy Siddons manhunt, the escalating tension was visibly evident. Everyone was keenly aware that to make good his escape, Siddons would not hesitate to kill again. They also knew he had the weapon smuggled in to him.

"Armed and Dangerous" was the caption under his picture on the flyers that were being distributed all over the city.

"Last time, we got two thousand useless tips, followed up every useless one of them, and the only reason we ever got him behind bars last summer was because he was dumb enough to hold up a gas station in Michigan while a cop was on the premises," Jack Shore growled to Mort Levy, as in disgust he watched a team of officers answer the flood of calls on the hot line.

Levy nodded absently. "Anything more about Siddons's girlfriend?" he asked Shore.

An hour ago one of the prisoners in Siddons's cellblock had told a guard that last month Siddons had bragged about a girlfriend named Paige, who he said was a world-class stripper.

They were trying to trace her in New York, but on the hunch that she might have been involved with Siddons in Michigan, Shore had contacted the authorities there.

"No, nothing so far. Probably another dead end."

"Call for you from Detroit, Jack," a voice bellowed above the din in the room. Both men turned quickly. In two strides Shore was at his desk and had grabbed the phone.

His caller did not waste time. "Stan Logan, Jack. We met when you came out to pick up Siddons last year. I may have something interesting for you."

"Let's have it."

"We never could find out where Siddons was hiding before he tried to pull the holdup here. The tip about Paige may be the answer. We've got a rap sheet on a Paige Laronde who calls herself an exotic dancer. She left town two days ago. Told a friend she didn't know if she'd be back, that she expected to join her boyfriend."

"Did she say where she was going?" Shore snapped.

"She said California, then Mexico."

"California and Mexico! Hell, if he makes it to Mexico we may never find him."

"Our guys are checking the train and bus stations as well as the airports, to see if we can pick up her trail. We'll keep you posted," Logan promised, then added, "We're about to fax her rap sheet and publicity pictures. Don't show them to your kids."

Shore slammed down the phone. "If Siddons managed to get out of New York this morning, he could be in California right now, maybe even Mexico."

"It would be pretty tough to get a plane reservation at the last minute on Christmas Eve," Levy reminded him cautiously.

"Listen, somebody got a gun in to him. That same somebody may have had clothes and cash and an airline ticket waiting for him. Probably managed to get him to an airport in Philadelphia or Boston, where no one's looking for him. My guess is that he's met up with his girlfriend by now and the two of them are heading south of the border, if they're not already eating enchiladas. And I still say one way or the other the go-between had to be Siddons's sister."

Frowning, Mort Levy watched Jack Shore go to the communications room to await the faxes from Detroit. The next step would be to forward pictures of both Siddons and his girlfriend to the border patrol in Tijuana, with the warning to be on the lookout for them.

But we still have to cover the cathedral tonight on the one-in-a-million chance that Jimmy's offer to surrender was on the level, Mort thought. Somehow neither possibility rang true to him—not Mexico, not the surrender. Would this Paige be smart enough to lie to her friend on the chance that the cops might come looking for her?

The coffee and sandwiches they had ordered were just being delivered. Mort went over to get his ham on rye. Two of the women officers were talking together.

He heard one of them, Lori Martini, say, "Still no sign of that missing kid. For sure some nut must have picked him up."

"What missing kid?" Levy asked.

Soberly he listened to the details. It was the one kind of case no one in the department could work on without becom-

ing emotionally involved. Mort had a seven-year-old son. He
knew what must be going through that mother's mind. And
the father so sick he hadn't even been told his son was missing. And all this at Christmastime. God, some people really
get it in spades, he thought.

"Call for you, Mort," a voice shouted from across the
room.

Carrying the coffee and sandwich, Mort returned to his
desk. "Who is it?" he asked as he took the receiver.

"A woman. She didn't give her name."

As Mort pressed the phone to his ear, he said, "Detective
Levy."

He heard the sound of frightened breathing. And then a
faint click as the line went dead.

WCBS reporter Alan Graham approached the squad car
where he'd interviewed Catherine Dornan an hour earlier
when he had done an update on the story.

It was eight-thirty, and the intermittent gusts of snow had
become a steady flow of large white flakes again.

Through his earphone, Graham heard the anchorman give
the latest information about the escaped prisoner. "The condition of Mario Bonardi, the injured prison guard, is still
extremely critical. Mayor Giuliani and Police Commissioner
Bratton have paid a second visit to the hospital where he is
in intensive care after delicate surgery. According to the latest
report, the police are following up on a tip that his assailant,
alleged murderer Jimmy Siddons, may be meeting a girlfriend
in California with the final destination, Mexico. The border
patrol at Tijuana has been alerted."

One of the newsmen had been tipped off that Jimmy's

lawyer claimed Siddons was turning himself in after midnight Mass at St. Patrick's. Alan Graham was glad that the decision had been made not to air that story. None of the police brass really believed it, and they didn't want the worshipers distracted by the rumor.

There were few pedestrians now on Fifth Avenue. It occurred to Graham that there was something almost obscene about the breaking stories they were covering this Christmas Eve: an escaped cop killer; a prison guard clinging to life; a seven-year-old missing boy, who was now the suspected victim of foul play.

He tapped on the window of the squad car. Catherine glanced up, then opened it halfway. Looking at her, he wondered how long she would be able to maintain her remarkable composure. She was sitting in the passenger seat of the car next to Officer Ortiz. Her son Michael was in the back with a handsome older woman whose arm was around him.

Catherine answered his unasked question. "I'm still waiting," she said quietly. "Officer Ortiz has been good enough to stay with me. I don't know why, but I feel as though somehow I'll find Brian right here." She turned slightly. "Mom, this is Alan Graham from WCBS. He interviewed me right after I spoke with you."

Barbara Cavanaugh saw the compassion on the face of the young reporter. Knowing that if there were anything to tell, they would have heard it by now, she still could not stop herself from asking, "Any word?"

"No, ma'am. We've had plenty of calls to the station, but they were all to express concern."

"He's vanished," Catherine said, her voice lifeless. "While Tom and I have raised the boys to basically trust people, they also know how to deal with emergencies. Brian knew enough to go to a policeman if he was lost. He knew to dial 911. Somebody has taken him. Who would take and hold a seven-year-old child unless . . . ?"

"Catherine, dear, don't torture yourself," her mother urged. "Everyone who heard you on the radio is praying for Brian. You must have faith."

Catherine felt frustration and anger rising inside her. Yes, she supposed she should have "faith." Certainly Brian had faith—he believed in that St. Christopher medal, probably enough to have followed whoever picked up my wallet. He knew it was inside, she reasoned, and felt he had to get it back. She looked back at her mother, and at Michael beside her. She felt her anger ebb. It wasn't her mother's fault that any of this had happened. No, faith—even in something as unlikely as a St. Christopher medal—was a good thing.

"You're right, Mom," she said.

From the receiver in his ear, Graham heard the anchorman say, "Over to you, Alan."

Stepping back from the car, he began, "Brian Dornan's mother is still keeping watch at the spot where her son disappeared shortly after 5:00 P.M. Authorities believe Catherine Dornan's theory that Brian may have seen someone steal her wallet and followed that person. The wallet contained a St. Christopher medal, which Brian was desperately anxious to bring to his father's hospital bed."

Graham handed the microphone to Catherine. "Brian believes the St. Christopher medal will help his father get well. If I had had Brian's faith, I would have guarded my wallet more carefully because the St. Christopher medal was in it. I want my husband to get better. I want my child," she said, her voice steady despite her emotion. "In the name of God, if anyone knows what happened to Brian, who has him, or where he is, please, *please* call us."

Graham stepped back from the squad car. "If anyone who knows anything about Brian's whereabouts is listening to that young mother's pain, we beg you to call this number, 212-555-0748."

11

Her eyes filled with tears, her lip quivering, Cally turned off the radio. *If anyone knows what happened to Brian . . .*

I *tried*, she told herself fiercely. I tried. She had dialed Detective Levy's number, but when she heard his voice, the enormity of what she was about to do overwhelmed her. They would arrest her. They would take Gigi away from her again and would put her with a new foster family. *If anyone knows anything about Brian's whereabouts . . .*

She reached for the phone.

From inside the bedroom she heard a wail and spun around. Gigi was having another nightmare. She rushed inside, sat down on the bed, gathered her child in her arms, and began rocking her. "Sshh, it's okay, everything's fine."

Gigi clung to her. "Mommy, Mommy. I dreamed that you were gone again. Please don't go, Mommy. Please don't leave me. I don't want to live with other people ever, ever."

"That won't happen, sweetheart, I promise."

She could feel Gigi relax. Gently she laid her back on

the pillow and smoothed her hair. "Now go back to sleep, angel."

Gigi closed her eyes, then opened them again. "Can I watch Santa Claus open his present?" she murmured.

Jimmy Siddons lowered the volume on the radio. "Your mom sure is flipping out about you, kid."

Brian had to keep himself from reaching out to the dashboard and touching the radio. Mom sounded so worried. He had to get back to her. Now she believed in the St. Christopher medal too. He was sure of it.

There were a lot of cars on the highway, and even though it was really snowing now, they were all going pretty fast. But Jimmy was in the far right lane, so no cars were coming up on that side. Brian began to plan.

If he could open the door real fast and roll out onto the road, he could keep rolling to the side. That way nobody would run over him. He pressed the medal for an instant, and then his hand crept to the handle on the door. When he put faint pressure on it, it moved slightly. He was right. Jimmy hadn't put the lock on after they stopped for gas.

Brian was about the throw open the door when he remembered his seat belt. He'd have to unfasten that just as the door swung open. Careful not to attract Jimmy's attention, he laid the index finger of his left hand on the seat belt's release button.

Just as Brian was about to pull on the handle and push the release, Jimmy swore. A car, weaving erratically, was coming up behind them on the left. An instant later it was so close it was almost touching the Toyota. Then it cut in front of them. Jimmy slammed on the brakes. The car skidded and fishtailed, as around them came the sound of metal impacting metal. Brian held his breath. Crash, he begged, *crash!* Then someone would help him.

But Jimmy righted the car and drove around the others. Just ahead, Brian could hear the wail of sirens and see the brilliance of flashing lights gathered around another accident, which they quickly drove past as well.

Jimmy grinned in savage satisfaction. "We're pretty lucky, aren't we, kiddo?" he asked Brian, as he glanced down at him.

Brian was still clutching the handle.

"Now you weren't thinking of jumping out if we'd gotten stuck back there, were you?" Jimmy asked. He clicked the control that locked the doors. "Keep your hand away from there. I see you touch that handle again and I'll break your fingers," he said quietly.

Brian didn't have the slightest doubt he would do just that.

12

It was five after ten. Mort Levy sat at his desk, deep in thought. He had only one explanation for the disconnected call: Cally Hunter. The tap from the police surveillance van outside Cally's building confirmed that she had dialed him. The men on duty there offered to go up and talk to her if Mort wanted them to. "No. Leave her alone," he ordered. He knew it would be pointless. She'd only repeat exactly what she'd told them before. But she knows something and she is afraid to tell, he thought. He had tried to phone her twice, but she had not answered. He knew she was there, though. The lookouts in the van would have notified them if she'd left the apartment. So why wasn't she answering? Should he go over to see her himself? Would it do any good?

"What's with you?" Jack Shore asked impatiently. "You forgot how to hear?"

Mort looked up. The rotund senior detective stood glowering down at him. No wonder Cally's afraid of you, Mort thought, remembering the fear in her eyes at Jack's anger and open hostility.

"I'm thinking," Mort said curtly, resisting the impulse to suggest that Shore try it sometime.

"Well, think with the rest of us. We've gotta go over the plans to cover the cathedral." Then Shore's scowl softened. "Mort, why don't you take a break?"

He isn't as bad as he tries to seem, Mort thought. "I don't see you taking a break, Jack," he replied.

"It's just that I hate Siddons worse than you do."

Mort got up slowly. His mind was still focused on the elusive memory of some important clue that had been overlooked, something he knew was there, right in front of him, but that he just couldn't make himself see. They'd seen Cally Hunter at seven-fifteen this morning. She'd already been dressed for work. They had seen her again nearly twelve hours later. She looked exhausted and desperately worried. She was probably in bed asleep now. But every nerve in his body was telling him that he should talk to her. Despite her denial, he believed she held the key.

As he turned away from his desk, the phone rang. When he picked it up, he again heard the terrified breathing. This time he took the initiative. "Cally," Mort said urgently. "Cally, *talk* to me. Don't be afraid. Whatever it is, I'll try to help you."

Cally could not even think of going to bed. She had listened to the all-news station, hoping but at the same time fearing that the cops had found Jimmy, praying that little Brian was safe.

At ten o'clock she had turned on the television to watch the Fox local news, then her heart sank. Brian's mother was seated next to the anchorman, Tony Potts. Her hair seemed looser now, as though she'd been standing outside in the wind and snow. Her face was very pale, and her eyes were filled with pain. There was a boy sitting next to her who seemed to be about ten or eleven years old.

The anchorman was saying, "You may have heard Catherine Dornan's appeals for help in finding her son Brian. We've asked her and Brian's brother, Michael, to be with us now. There were crowds of people on Fifth Avenue and Forty-ninth Street shortly after five o'clock this evening. Maybe you were one of them. Maybe you noticed Catherine with her two sons, Michael and Brian. They were in a group listening to a violinist playing Christmas carols, and singing along. Seven-year-old Brian disappeared from his mother's side. His mother and brother need your help in finding him."

The anchorman turned to Catherine. "You're holding a picture of Brian."

Cally watched as the picture was held up, listened as Brian's mother said, "It's not very clear, so let me tell you a little more about him. He's seven but looks younger because he's small. He has dark reddish brown hair and blue eyes and freckles on his nose . . ." Her voice faltered.

Cally shut her eyes. She couldn't bear to look at the stark agony on Catherine Dornan's face.

Michael put his hand over his mother's. "My brother's wearing a dark blue ski jacket just like mine, 'cept mine is green, and a red cap. And one of his front teeth is missing." Then he burst out, "We gotta get him back. We can't tell my Dad that Brian is missing. Dad's too sick to be worried."

Michael's voice became even more urgent. "I know my dad. He'd try to do something. He'd get out of bed and start looking for Brian, and we can't let him do that. He's sick, real sick."

Cally snapped off the set. She tiptoed into the bedroom where Gigi was at last sleeping peacefully and went over to the window that led to the fire escape. She could still see Brian's eyes as he glanced over his shoulder, begging her to help him, his one hand in Jimmy's grasp, his other holding the St. Christopher medal as though it would somehow save him. She shook her head. That medal, she thought. He hadn't cared about the money. He followed her because he believed that medal would make his father get well.

Cally ran the few steps back into the living room and grabbed Mort Levy's card.

When he answered, her resolve almost crumbled again, but then his voice was so kind when he said, "Cally, *talk* to me. Don't be afraid."

"Mr. Levy," she blurted out, "can you come here, quick? I've *got* to talk to you about Jimmy—and that little boy who's missing."

13

All that was left of the snack Jimmy had purchased
when they stopped for gas were the empty Coca-
Cola cans and the crumpled bags that had held
potato chips. Jimmy had thrown his on the floor in front
of Brian, while Brian had placed his in the plastic waste-
basket attached under the dashboard. He couldn't even remember what the chips had tasted like. He was so hungry
that, scared as he felt, being hungry was all he could think
about.

He knew that Jimmy was really mad at him. And ever
since the time they'd nearly crashed and Jimmy realized that
he had been planning to try to jump out of the car, he'd
seemed real nervous. He kept opening and closing his fingers
on the steering wheel, making a scary snapping sound. The
first time he did it, Brian had flinched and jumped, and Jimmy
had grabbed him by the shoulder, snarling at him to stay
away from the door.

The snow was coming down faster now. Ahead of them

someone braked. The car swung around in a circle, then kept going. Brian realized that it hadn't slammed into another car only because all the drivers on the road were trying to keep from getting too close to other cars.

Even so, Jimmy began to swear, a low steady stream of words, most of which Brian had never heard, even from Skeet, the kid in his class who knew all the good swear words.

The spinning car confirmed Jimmy's growing sense that near as he was to escaping the country something could still go wrong any minute. It didn't sound as though that prison guard he shot was going to make it. If the guard died . . . Jimmy had meant it when he told Cally that they wouldn't take him alive.

Then Jimmy tried to reassure himself. He had a car that probably nobody even realized was missing yet. He had decent clothes and money. If they'd been stuck back there when that crazy fool caused the accident, the kid might have managed to jump out of the car. If that jerk who just spun around had hit the Toyota, I might have been hurt, Jimmy thought. On my own, maybe I could've bluffed it, but not with the kid along. On the other hand, nobody knew he had the kid, and in a million years no cop was on the lookout for a guy in a nice car with a bunch of toys in the backseat and a little boy beside him.

They were near Syracuse now. In three or four hours he'd be across the border with Paige.

There was a McDonald's sign on the right. Jimmy was hungry, and this would be a good place to get something to eat. It would have to last him until he reached Canada. He'd pull up to the drive-in window, order for the two of them, then get back on the road fast.

"What's your favorite food, kid?" he asked, his tone almost genial.

Brian had spotted the McDonald's sign and held his breath, hoping that this meant they were going to get something to eat. "A hamburger and french fries, and a Coke," he said timidly.

"If I stop at McDonald's, can you look like you're sleeping?"

"Yes, I promise."

"Do it then. Lean against me with your eyes closed."

"Okay." Obediently Brian slumped against Jimmy and squeezed his eyes shut. He tried not to show how scared he was.

"Let's see what kind of actor you are," Jimmy said. "And you'd better be good."

The St. Christopher medal had slipped to the side. Brian straightened it so that he could feel it, heavy and comforting against his chest.

It was scary to be so close to this guy, not like being sleepy when he was driving with Dad and curling up against him and feeling Dad's hand patting his shoulder.

Jimmy pulled off the highway. They had to wait on line at the drive-in window. Jimmy froze when he saw a state trooper pull in behind them, but had no choice except to stay put and not draw attention to himself. When it was their turn and he placed the order and paid, the attendant didn't even glance into the car. But at the pickup spot, the woman looked over the counter to where the light from behind her shone on Brian.

"I guess he just can't wait to see what Santa Claus is going to bring him, can he?"

Jimmy nodded and tried to smile in agreement as he reached for the bag.

She leaned way forward and peered into the car. "My goodness, is he wearing a St. Christopher medal? My dad was named after him and used to try to make a big deal of it, but my mom always jokes about St. Christopher being dropped from the calendar of saints. My dad says it's too bad Mom wasn't named Philomena. She's another saint the Vatican said didn't exist." With a hearty laugh the young woman handed over the bag.

As they drove back onto the highway, Brian opened his eyes. He could smell the hamburgers and the french fries. He sat up slowly.

Jimmy looked at him, his eyes steely, his face rigid. Through lips that barely parted, he quietly ordered, "Get that goddamn medal off your neck."

Cally had to talk to him about her brother and the missing child. After promising to be right over, Mort Levy hung up the phone, stunned. What possible connection could there be between Jimmy Siddons and the little boy who disappeared on Fifth Avenue?

He dialed the lookout van. "You recorded that call?"

"Is she crazy, Mort? She can't be talking about the Dornan kid, can she? Want us to pick her up for questioning?"

"That's just what I *don't* want you to do!" Levy exploded. "She's scared to death as it is. Sit tight until I get there."

He had to inform his superiors, starting with Jack Shore, about Cally Hunter's call. Mort spotted Shore leaving the chief of detectives' private office, was out of his chair and across the room in seconds. He grabbed Shore's arm. "Come back inside."

"I told you to take a break." Shore tried to shake off his hand. "We just heard from Logan in Detroit again. Two days ago a woman whose description matches Siddons's girlfriend got a ride from a private car service over the border to Windsor. Logan's guys think that Laronde told her girlfriend about California and Mexico to throw them off her trail. The girlfriend was questioned again. This time it occurred to her to mention that she offered to buy Laronde's fur coat because it wouldn't be needed in Mexico. Laronde refused."

I never bought that Mexico story, Mort Levy thought. He didn't relinquish his grip on Shore's arm as he shoved open the chief's door.

Five minutes later, a squad car was racing up the East Side Drive to Avenue B and Tenth Street. A bitterly frustrated Jack Shore had been ordered to wait in the lookout van while Mort and the chief, Bud Folney, went upstairs to talk to Cally.

Mort knew that Shore would not forgive him for insisting that he stay out of it. "Jack, when we were there earlier, I knew there was something she was holding back. You've scared her to death. She thinks you'd do anything to see her back behind bars. For God's sake, can't you look at her as a human being? She's got a four-year-old child, her husband is dead, and she got the book thrown at her when she made the mistake of helping the brother she'd practically raised."

Now Mort turned to Folney. "I don't know how Jimmy Siddons ties into that missing child, but I do know that Cally has been too frightened to talk. If she tells us now whatever she knows, it will be because she feels that the department . . . you . . . aren't out to get her."

Folney nodded. He was a soft-spoken, lean man in his late forties, with a scholarly face. He had in fact spent three years as a high school teacher before realizing his passion was law enforcement. It was widely believed among the ranks that one day he'd be police commissioner. Already he was one of the most powerful men in the department.

Mort Levy knew that if there was anyone who could help Cally, assuming she had in some way been forced to cover for Jimmy again, it was Folney. But the missing child—how could Siddons be involved in this?

It was a question they were all frantic to ask.

When the squad car pulled up behind the surveillance van, Shore made one last appeal. "If I keep my mouth shut . . ."

Folney answered, "I suggest you start right now, Jack. Get in the van."

14

Pete Cruise had been about to call it a day. He'd discovered where Cally Hunter lived when he tried to interview her after she was released from prison, and now he was hoping her brother would show up. But there'd been nothing to watch for hours except the on-again-off-again falling snow. Now at least it seemed to have stopped for good. The van that he knew was a police van was still parked across the street from Cally's apartment, but probably all they were doing was monitoring her calls. The likelihood of Jimmy Siddons suddenly showing up at his sister's house now was about the same as two strangers having matching DNA.

All the hours of hanging around Hunter's building were a waste, Pete decided. From the time he'd seen Cally come home shortly before six, and the two detectives stop in around seven, it had been a big nothing.

He'd kept his powerful portable radio on the whole time he waited, switching between the police band, his station,

WYME, and the WCBS news station. No word of Siddons at all. Shame about that missing kid.

When the ten o'clock news came on WYME, Pete thought for the hundredth time that the anchor in that slot sounded like a wimp. But she did have some real emotion when she talked about the missing seven-year-old. Maybe we need a missing kid every day, Pete thought sarcastically, then was immediately ashamed of himself.

There was a lot of activity in Hunter's building, people coming and going. Many of the churches had moved up the midnight services to ten o'clock. No matter what time they schedule them, some people will always be late, Pete thought as he saw an elderly couple hurry from the building and turn up Avenue B. Probably heading for St. Emeric's.

The woman who had brought Hunter's kid home earlier was coming up the block. Was she headed for Hunter's apartment? Cally planning to go out? he wondered.

Pete shrugged. Maybe Hunter had a late date or was going to church herself. Obviously, today wasn't the day to get the story that was going to make his name as a reporter.

It'll happen, Pete promised himself. I won't always be working on this lousy ten-watt station. His buddy who worked at WNBC loved to ride Pete about his job. A favorite put-down was that the only audience for WYME were two cockroaches and three stray cats. "This is station Why-Me," he'd joke.

Pete started his car. He was just about to pull out when a squad car raced down the block and stopped in front of Cally's building.

Through narrowed eyes, Pete observed three men emerge.

One he recognized as Jack Shore crossed the street and got into the van. Then in the light from the building entrance he could make out Mort Levy. He didn't get a good look at the other one.

Something was breaking. Pete turned off the engine, suddenly interested again.

While she waited for Mort Levy, Cally took Gigi's Christmas presents from their hiding place behind the couch and set them in front of the tree. The secondhand doll's carriage didn't look that bad, she decided, with the pretty blue satin coverlet and pillowcase. She'd put the baby doll she'd picked up for a couple of dollars last month in it, but it wasn't nearly as cute as the one that she'd wanted to buy from the peddler on Fifth Avenue. That one had Gigi's golden-brown hair and was wearing a blue party dress. *If she hadn't been looking for that peddler, she wouldn't have seen the wallet, and the boy wouldn't have followed her, and . . .*

She put that thought aside. She was past feeling now. Carefully, she stacked the presents she'd wrapped with candy-cane paper: an outfit from The Gap—leggings and a polo shirt; crayons and a coloring book; some furniture for Gigi's dollhouse. Everything, even the two pieces of the Gap outfit, was in separate boxes so at least it looked as though Gigi had a stack of gifts to open.

She tried to avoid looking at the largest package under the tree, the package that Gigi thought was their gift for Santa Claus.

Finally she phoned Aika. Aika's grandchildren always went home to sleep, so she was sure she could come over and stay with Gigi in case the cops arrested Cally after she told them about Jimmy and the little boy.

Aika answered on the first ring. "Hello." Her voice was filled with her normal warmth. If only they'd let Gigi stay with Aika if they put me in prison again, Cally thought. She swallowed over the lump in her throat, then said, "Aika, I'm in trouble. Can you come over in about half an hour and maybe stay overnight?"

"You bet I can." Aika did not ask questions, simply clicked off.

As Cally replaced the receiver, the buzzer from the downstairs door resounded through the apartment.

"The switchboard's on fire, Mrs. Dornan," Leigh Ann Winick, the producer of Fox 5 Ten O'clock News told Catherine as, carefully avoiding the floor cables, she and Michael left the broadcast area. "It looks as though everyone in our viewing area wants you to know that they're rooting and praying for Brian and your husband."

"Thank you." Catherine tried to smile. She looked down at Michael. He had been trying so hard to keep up his spirits for her sake. It was only when she had listened to his on-camera plea that she had fully realized what this was doing to him.

Michael's hands were in his pockets, his shoulders hunched under his ears. It was exactly the same posture Tom unconsciously fell into when he was worried about a patient. Catherine squared her own shoulders and put her arm around her older son as the door from the studio closed behind them.

The producer said, "Our operators are thanking everyone in your name, but is there anything else you'd like us to tell our audience?"

Catherine drew a deep breath, and her arm tightened around Michael. "I wish you'd tell them that we think I dropped my wallet, and that Brian apparently followed whoever picked it up. The reason he was so anxious to get it back is that my mother had just given me a St. Christopher medal that my father wore through World War II. My father believed the medal kept him safe. It even has a dent where a bullet glanced off it, a bullet that might have killed him. Brian has the same wonderful faith that St. Christopher or what he represents is going to take care of us again . . . and so do I. St. Christopher will carry Brian back to us on his shoulders, and he will help my husband get well."

She smiled down at Michael. "Right, pal?"

Michael's eyes were shining. "Mom, do you really believe that?"

Catherine drew a deep breath. *I believe, Lord, help my unbelief.* "Yes, I do," she said firmly.

And maybe because it was Christmas Eve, for the first time, she really did.

15

State Trooper Chris McNally tuned out as Deidre Lenihan droned on about just seeing a St. Christopher medal, and how her father was named after St. Christopher. She was a well-meaning young woman, but every time he stopped for coffee at this McDonald's, she seemed to be on duty and always wanted to talk.

Tonight Chris was too preoccupied with thoughts of getting home. He wanted to get at least some sleep before his kids got up to open all their Christmas presents. He also had been thinking about the Toyota he had just seen pull out in front of him. He'd been thinking of buying one himself, although he knew his wife wouldn't want a brown one. A new car meant monthly payments to worry about. He noticed the remnant of a bumper sticker on the Toyota, a single word, *inheritance*. He knew the sticker had originally said, "We're spending our grandchildren's inheritance." We could use an inheritance, he thought.

"And my father said . . ."

Chris forced himself to refocus. Deidre's nice, he thought, but she talks too much. He reached for the bag she was dangling in her hand, but it was clear she was not going to relinquish it yet, not until she had told how her dad said it was too bad that her mother hadn't been named Philomena.

Still she wasn't finished. "Years ago my aunt worked in Southampton and belonged to St. Philomena's parish. When they had to rename it, the pastor had a contest to decide which saint they should choose and why. My aunt suggested St. Dymphna because she said she was the saint of the insane and most of the people in the parish were nuts."

"Well, I was named after St. Christopher myself," Chris said, managing to snare the bag. "Merry Christmas, Deidre."

And it will be Christmas before I get a bite out of this Big Mac, he thought as he drove back onto the Thruway. With one hand, he deftly opened the bag, freed the burger, and gratefully took a large bite. The coffee would have to wait until he got back to his post.

He'd be off duty at midnight, and then, he thought, smiling to himself, it would be time to grab a little shut-eye. Eileen would try to keep the kids in bed till six, but lots of luck. It hadn't happened last year and it wouldn't happen this year if he knew his sons.

He was approaching exit 40 and drove the car to the official turnaround, from which he could observe errant drivers. Christmas Eve was nothing like New Year's Eve for nabbing drinkers, but Chris was determined that no one who was speeding or weaving on the road was going to get past him. He'd witnessed a couple of accidents where some drunk turned the holiday into a nightmare for innocent people. Not tonight if he could help it. And the snow had made driving that much more treacherous.

As Chris opened the lid on his coffee, he frowned. A Corvette doing at least eighty was racing up the service lane. He snapped on his dome lights and siren, shifted into gear, and the squad car leaped in pursuit.

Chief of Detectives Bud Folney listened with no expression other than quiet attentiveness as a trembling Cally Hunter told Mort Levy about finding the wallet on Fifth Avenue. She had waived her Miranda warning, saying impatiently, "This can't wait any longer."

Folney knew the basics of her case: older sister of Jimmy Siddons, had served time because a judge had not believed her story that she thought she was helping her brother get away from a rival gang bent on killing him. Levy had told him that Hunter seemed to be one of the hard-luck people of this world—raised by an elderly grandmother, who died, leaving her to try to straighten out her louse of a younger brother when she was only a kid herself; then her husband killed by a hit-and-run driver when she was pregnant.

About thirty, Folney thought, and could be pretty with a little meat on her. She still had the pale, haunted expression he had seen on other women who had been imprisoned and carried with them the horror that someday they might be sent back.

He looked around. The neat apartment, the sunny, yellow paint on the cracked walls, the bravely decorated but skimpy Christmas tree, the new coverlet on the battered doll carriage, they all told him something about Cally Hunter.

Folney knew that, like himself, Mort Levy was desperate to know what connection Hunter could give them between Siddons and the missing Dornan child. He approved of Mort's gentle approach. Cally Hunter had to tell it her way. It's a good thing we didn't bring in the raging bull, Folney thought. Jack Shore was a good detective, but his aggressiveness often got on Folney's nerves.

Hunter was talking about seeing the wallet on the sidewalk. "I picked it up without thinking. I guessed it belonged to that woman, but I wasn't sure. I honestly wasn't sure," she burst out, "and I thought if I tried to give it back to her, she might say something was missing from it. That happened to my grandmother. And then you'd send me back to prison and . . ."

"Cally, take it easy," Mort said. "What happened then?"

"When I got home . . ."

She told them about finding Jimmy in the apartment, wearing her deceased husband's clothes. She pointed to the big package under the tree. "The guard's uniform and coat are in there," she said. "It was the only place I could think to hide them in case you came back."

That's it, Mort thought. When we looked around the apartment the second time, there was something different about the closet. The box on the shelf and the man's jacket were missing.

Cally's voice became ragged and uneven as she told them about Jimmy taking Brian Dornan and threatening to kill him if he spotted a cop chasing him.

Levy asked, "Cally, do you think Jimmy can be trusted to let Brian go?"

"I wanted to think so," she said tonelessly. "That was

what I told myself when I didn't call you immediately. But I know he's desperate. Jimmy will do anything to keep from going to prison again."

Folney finally asked a question. "Cally, why did you call us now?"

"I saw Brian's mother on television, and I knew that if Jimmy had taken Gigi, I'd want you to help me get her back." Cally clasped her hands together. Her body swayed slightly forward then back in the ancient posture of grief. "The look on that little boy's face, the way he put that medal around his neck and was holding on to it like it was a life preserver . . . if anything happens to him, it's my fault."

The buzzer sounded. If that's Shore . . . Folney thought as he jumped up to answer it.

It was Aika Banks. When she entered the apartment, she looked at the policemen searchingly, then rushed to Cally and hugged her. "Baby, what is it? What's wrong? Why do you need me to stay with Gigi? What do these people want?"

Cally winced in pain.

Aika peeled up her friend's sleeve. The bruises caused by Jimmy's fingers were now an ugly purple. Any doubts that Bud Folney had about Hunter's possible cooperation with her brother disappeared. He squatted in front of her. "Cally, you're not going to get into trouble. I promise you. I believe you found that wallet. I believe you didn't know what was best for you to do. But now you've got to help us. *Have you any idea where Jimmy might have gone?*"

Ten minutes later, when they left Cally's apartment, Mort Levy was carrying the bulky gift-wrapped package that held the guard's uniform.

Shore joined them in the squad car and impatiently fired questions at Mort. As they were driven downtown, they agreed that the search for Jimmy Siddons would be based on the assumption that he might be trying to reach Canada.

"He's got to be in a car," Folney said flatly. "There's no way he'll travel on public transportation with that child."

Cally had told them that from the time he was twelve years old, Jimmy could hot-wire and steal any car; she was sure he must have had one waiting near the apartment.

"My guess is that Siddons would want to get out of New York State as soon as possible," Folney said. "Which means he'd drive through New England to the border. But it's only a guess. He could be on the Thruway, headed for I87. That's the fastest route."

And Siddons's girlfriend was probably in Canada. It all fit together.

They also accepted Cally's absolute certainty that Jimmy Siddons would not be taken alive and that his final act of vengeance would be to kill his hostage.

So they were faced with an escaped murderer with a child, possibly driving a car they could not describe, probably headed north in a snowstorm. It would be like looking for a needle in a haystack. Siddons would be too smart to attract attention by speeding. The border was always mobbed with holiday traffic on Christmas Eve. He dictated a message to be sent to state police throughout New England as well as New York. "Has threatened to kill the hostage," he emphasized.

They calculated that if Siddons had left Cally Hunter's apartment shortly after six, depending on driving conditions, he'd be between two and three hundred miles away. The alert that went out to the state police contained Cally's final certainty: *On a chain around his neck, the child may be wearing a bronze St. Christopher medal the size of a silver dollar.*

Pete Cruise watched as the detectives emerged from Cally Hunter's building some twenty minutes after arriving there. He noted that Levy was carrying a bulky package. Shore immediately jumped out of the van and joined them.

This time Pete got a good look at the third man, then whistled silently. It was Bud Folney, chief of detectives and in line to be the next police commissioner. Something was breaking. Something big.

The squad car took off with its dome light flashing. A block away its siren was turned on. Pete sat for a moment, debating what to do. The cops in the van might stop him if he tried to go in to see Cally, but obviously something major was going down here, and he was determined to scoop everyone on this.

As he was wondering about looking for a back entrance to the building, he saw the woman he knew to be Cally's babysitter leave. In a flash he was out of the car and following her. He caught up with her when she turned the corner and they were out of sight of the cops in the van. "I'm Detective Cruise," he said. "I've been instructed to see you safely home. How is Cally doing?"

"Oh, that poor girl," Aika began. "Officer, you people have to believe her. She thought she was doing the right thing when she didn't phone you about her brother kidnapping that little boy . . ."

. . .

Even though Brian was hungry, the hamburger was hard to swallow. His throat felt like there was something stuck in it. He knew that Jimmy was the reason for that. He took a giant swallow of Coke and tried to think about how Daddy would beat Jimmy up for being so mean to him.

But now when he thought about Daddy it was hard to remember anything except all the plans they had made for Christmas Eve. Daddy had planned to come home early, and they were all going to trim the tree together. Then they were going to have dinner and go around their neighborhood singing Christmas carols with a bunch of their friends.

That was all he could think about now, because that was all he wanted, to be home and have Daddy and Mommy smiling a lot the way they always did when they were together. When they came to New York because Dad was sick, Mom had told him and Michael that their big presents, the ones they really wanted, would be waiting for them when they got back home. She said that Santa Claus would keep the presents on his sleigh until he knew they were in their own house again.

Michael had said, "Yeah, really," under his breath to Brian. But Brian believed in Santa Claus. Last year Dad had pointed out marks on the roof of the garage where Santa's sleigh had landed and where the reindeer had stood. Michael told him he heard Mom tell Dad it was a good thing Dad hadn't broken his neck sliding around on the icy roof and making tracks all over it, but Brian didn't mind what Michael said, because he didn't believe it. Just like he didn't mind that Michael sometimes called him the Dork; he knew he wasn't a dork.

He knew things were bad when you wished your jerk

brother, who could be such a pain in the neck, was there with you, and that was just how he felt now.

As Brian swallowed over that feeling of something in his throat, the plastic container almost jumped out of his hand. He realized Jimmy had switched lanes fast.

Jimmy Siddons swore silently. He had just passed a state trooper's car stopped in back of a sports car. The sight of a trooper made him sweat all over, but he shouldn't have switched lanes like that. He was getting jumpy.

Sensing the animosity that bristled from Jimmy, Brian put the uneaten hamburger and the soda back in the bag and, moving slowly so Jimmy could see what he was doing, leaned down and put the bag on the floor. Then he straightened up, huddled against the back of the seat and hugged his arms against his sides. The fingers of his right hand groped until they closed around the St. Christopher medal, which he had laid on the seat next to him when he opened the package of food.

With a sense of relief he closed his hand over it and mentally pictured the strong saint who carried the little kid across the dangerous river, who had taken care of his grandfather, who would make Dad get better and who . . . Brian closed his eyes . . . He didn't finish the wish, but in his mind he could see himself on the shoulders of the saint.

16

Barbara Cavanaugh was waiting for Catherine and Michael in the green room at Channel 5. "You both did a great job," she said quietly. Then, seeing the exhaustion on her daughter's face, she said, "Catherine, please come back to the apartment. The police will get in touch with you there as soon as they have any word about Brian. You look ready to drop."

"I can't, Mother," Catherine said. "I know it's foolish to wait on Fifth Avenue. Brian isn't going to get back there on his own, but while I'm out and about I at least feel as though I'm doing something to find him. I don't really know what I'm saying except that when I left your apartment, I had my two little boys with me, and when I go back they're going to be with me, too."

Leigh Ann Winick made a decision. "Mrs. Dornan, why not stay right here at least for the present? This room is comfortable. We'll send out for some hot soup or a sandwich or whatever you want. But you've said yourself, there's no point in just waiting on Fifth Avenue indefinitely."

Catherine considered. "And the police will be able to reach me here?"

Winick pointed to the phone. "Absolutely. Now tell me what I can order for you."

Twenty minutes later, as Catherine, her mother, and Michael were sipping steaming hot minestrone, they watched the green room's television monitor. The news bite was about Mario Bonardi, the wounded prison guard. Although still critical, his condition had stabilized.

The reporter was with Bonardi's wife and teenage children in the waiting room of the intensive care unit. When asked for a comment, a weary Rose Bonardi said, "My husband is going to make it. I want to thank everyone who has been praying for him today. Our family has known many happy Christmases, but this will be the best ever because we know what we so nearly lost."

"That's what we'll be saying, Michael," Catherine said determinedly. "Dad is going to make it and Brian is going to be found."

The reporter with the Bonardi family said, "Back to you at the news desk, Tony."

"Thanks, Ted. Glad to hear that it's going so well. That's the kind of Christmas story we want to be able to tell." The anchor's smile vanished. "There is still no trace of Mario Bonardi's assailant, Jimmy Siddons, who was awaiting trial for the murder of a police officer. Police sources are quoted as saying that he may be planning to meet his girlfriend, Paige Laronde, in Mexico. Airports, train stations, and bus terminals are under heavy surveillance. It was nearly three years ago, while making his escape after an armed robbery, that Siddons shot and fatally wounded Officer William

Grasso, who had stopped him for a traffic violation. Siddons is known to be armed and should be considered extremely dangerous."

As the anchorman spoke, Jimmy Siddons's mug shots were flashed on the screen.

"He looks mean," Michael observed as he studied the cold eyes and sneering lips of the escaped prisoner.

"He certainly does," Barbara Cavanaugh agreed. Then she looked at her grandson's face. "Mike, why don't you close your eyes and rest for a little while?" she suggested.

He shook his head. "I don't want to go to sleep."

It was one minute of eleven. The newscaster was saying, "In an update, we have no further information about the whereabouts of seven-year-old Brian Dornan, who has been missing since shortly after five o'clock today.

"On this very special evening, we ask you to continue to pray that Brian is safely returned to his family, and wish you and all of your loved ones a very Merry Christmas."

In an hour it will be Christmas, Catherine thought. *Brian, you have to come back, you have to be found. You have to be with me in the morning when we go see Dad. Brian, come back. Please come back.*

The door of the green room opened. Winick ushered in a tall man in his late forties, followed by Officer Manuel Ortiz. "Detective Rhodes wants to talk to you, Mrs. Dornan," Winick said. "I'm outside if you need me."

Catherine saw the grave look on the faces of both Rhodes and Ortiz, and fear paralyzed her. She was unable to move or speak.

They realized what she was thinking. "No, Mrs. Dornan, it isn't that," Ortiz said quickly.

Rhodes took over. "I'm from headquarters, Mrs. Dornan. We have information about Brian, but let me begin by saying that as far as we know he's alive and unharmed."

"Then where is he?" Michael burst out. 'Where's my brother?"

Catherine listened as Detective Rhodes explained about her wallet being picked up by a young woman who was the sister of escaped prisoner Jimmy Siddons. Her mind did not want to accept that Brian had been abducted by the murderer whose face she had just seen on the television screen. No, she thought, no, that can't be.

She pointed to the monitor. "They just reported that that man is probably on his way to Mexico. Brian disappeared six hours ago. He could be in Mexico right now."

"At headquarters we don't buy that story," Rhodes told her. "We think he's heading for Canada, probably in a stolen car. We're concentrating the search in that direction."

Suddenly Catherine could feel no emotion. It was like when she was in the delivery room and was given the shot of Demerol and all the pain miraculously stopped. *And she'd looked up to see Tom wink at her. Tom, always there for her. "Feels better doesn't it, Babe?" he had asked. And her mind, no longer clouded with pain, had become so clear.* It was that way now, as well. "What kind of car are they in?"

Rhodes looked uncomfortable. "We don't know," he said. "We're only guessing that he's in a car, but we feel sure it's the right guess. We have every trooper throughout New York and New England on the alert for a man traveling with a young boy who is wearing a St. Christopher medal."

"Brian is wearing the medal?" Michael exclaimed. "Then

he'll be all right. Gran, tell Mom that the medal will take care of Brian like it took care of Grandpa."

"Armed and dangerous," Catherine repeated.

"Mrs. Dornan," Rhodes said urgently. "If Siddons is in a car, he's probably listening to the radio. He's smart. Now that Officer Bonardi is out of danger, Siddons knows he isn't facing a death sentence. Capital punishment had not been reinstated when he killed the police officer three years ago. And he did tell his sister that he'd let Brian go tomorrow morning."

Her mind was so clear. "But you don't believe that, do you?"

She did not need to see the expression on his face to know that Detective Rhodes did not believe that Jimmy Siddons would voluntarily release Brian.

"Mrs. Dornan, if we're right and Siddons is heading for the Canadian border, he's not going to get there for at least another three or four hours. Although the snow has stopped in some areas, the roads are still going to be something of a mess all night. He can't be traveling fast, and he doesn't know that we know he has Brian. That's being kept from the media. In Siddons's mind, Brian will be an asset—at least until he reaches the border. We will find him before then."

The television monitor was still on with the volume low. Catherine's back was to it. She saw Detective Rhodes's face change, heard a voice say, "We interrupt this program for a news bulletin. According to a report that has just been broadcast by station WYME, seven-year-old Brian Dornan, the boy who has been missing since this afternoon, has fallen into the hands of alleged murderer Jimmy Siddons, who told his sister that if the police close in on him, he will put a bullet through the child's head. More later, as news comes in."

17

After Aika left, Cally made a cup of tea, wrapped herself in a blanket, turned the television on, and pressed the MUTE button. This way I'll know if there's any news, she thought. Then she turned on the radio and tuned in a station playing Christmas music, but she kept the volume low.

"*Hark, the herald angels sing . . .*" Remember how Frank and I sang that together when we were trimming the tree? she thought. Five years ago. Their one Christmas together. They'd just learned that she was pregnant. She remembered all the plans they'd made. "Next year we'll have help trimming the tree," Frank had said.

"Sure we will. A three-month-old baby will be a big help," she'd said, laughing.

She remembered Frank lifting her up so that she could place the star on the top of the tree.

Why?

Why had everything gone so wrong? There wasn't a next year. Just one week later Frank was killed by a hit-and-run driver. He'd been on his way home from a trip to the deli for a carton of milk.

We had so little time, Cally thought, shaking her head. Sometimes she wondered if those months were just a dream. It seemed so long ago now.

"*O come, all ye faithful, joyful and triumphant . . .*" "Adeste Fideles." Was it just yesterday that I was feeling so good about life? Cally wondered. At work the hospital administrator had said, "Cally, I've been hearing wonderful reports on you. They tell me you've got the makings of a born nurse. Have you ever thought of going to nursing school?" Then she'd talked about scholarships and how she was going to look into it.

That little boy, Cally thought. Oh God, don't let Jimmy hurt him. I should have called Detective Levy immediately. I know I should have. Why didn't I? she wondered, then immediately answered her own question: Because I wasn't just afraid for Brian. I was afraid for myself, too, and that may cost Brian his life.

She got up and went in to look at Gigi. As usual, the little girl had managed to work one foot out from under the covers. She did it every night, even when the room was cold.

Cally tucked the covers around her daughter's shoulders, then touched the small foot and tucked that in, too. Gigi stirred. "Mommy," she said drowsily.

"I'm right here."

Cally went back to the living room and glanced over at the television for a moment, then rushed to turn up the volume. No! No! she thought as she heard the reporter explain that police now had information that the missing boy had been kidnapped by escaped cop killer Jimmy Siddons. The police will blame the leak on me, she thought frantically. They'll think I told someone. I know they will.

The phone rang. When she picked it up and heard Mort Levy's voice, the pent-up emotions that had seemed so frozen erupted suddenly. "I didn't do it," she sobbed. "I didn't tell anyone. I swear, I swear I didn't tell."

The steady rise and fall of Brian's chest told Jimmy Siddons that his hostage was asleep. Good, he thought, better for me. The problem was that the kid was smart. Smart enough to know that if he had managed to throw himself out of the car next to the breakdown lane, he wouldn't risk getting run over. If that jerk hadn't spun out and caused the fender-bender, it would be all over for me now, Jimmy thought. The kid would have gotten out and the troopers would have been on my tail right then.

It was past eleven o'clock. The kid should be tired. With luck he'd sleep for a couple of hours anyhow. Even with the snow on the roads, they should be at the border in, at most, three or four hours. It'll still be dark for a long time after that, Jimmy thought with satisfaction. He knew he could count on Paige to be waiting on the Canadian side. They'd worked out a rendezvous point in the woods about three miles from the customs check.

Jimmy debated about where he should leave the Toyota. There was nothing to tie him to it as long as he made sure he wiped it clean of fingerprints. Maybe he'd ditch it in one of the wooded areas.

On the other hand . . . He thought of the Niagara River, where he would make the border crossing. It had a strong current, so chances were it wouldn't be frozen. With luck, the car might never surface.

What about the kid? Even as he asked himself the question, Jimmy knew there was no way he'd take a chance on the kid being found near the border and able to talk about him.

Paige had told all her friends she was going to Mexico.

Sorry, kid, Jimmy thought. That's where I want the cops looking for me.

He reflected for a moment, then decided the river would take care of the car *and* the kid.

That decision made, Jimmy felt some of the tension ease from his body. With every mile, he felt more sure that he was going to make it, that Canada and Paige and freedom were within reach. And with each mile he felt more anxious—and more determined—that nothing happen to screw it up.

Like last time. He'd been all set. He'd had Cally's car, a hundred bucks, and was heading for California. Then he ran a lousy caution light on Ninth Avenue and got pulled over. The cop, a guy about thirty, thought he was a big shot. He had come to the driver's window and said real sarcastically, "Driver's license and registration, *sir*."

That's all he would have needed to see, Jimmy thought, remembering the moment as though it were yesterday, a license issued to James Siddons. He had had no choice. He would have been arrested on the spot. He'd reached into his breast pocket, pulled out his gun, and fired. Before the cop's body hit the ground, Jimmy was out of the car and on the street, blending into the crowd around the bus terminal. He had looked at the departure schedule board and rushed to buy a ticket on a bus leaving in three minutes, destination: Detroit.

That was a lucky decision, Jimmy thought. He'd met Paige the first night, moved in with her, then got some phony ID and a job with a low-life security firm. For a while he and Paige had even had a kind of normal life. Their only real arguments were when he got sore at the way she encouraged the guys who made passes at her in the strip joint. But she said it was her job to make them *want* to make passes at her. For the first time, everything was actually working out. Until he was dumb enough to hit the service station without taking enough time to case it.

He focused his attention back on the snow-covered road ahead of him. He could tell from the feel of the tires that it was getting icy. Good thing this car had snow tires, Jimmy thought. He flashed back to the couple who owned the car— what had the guy said to his wife? Something about can't wait to see Bobby's face? Yeah, that was it, Jimmy thought, grinning as he imagined their faces when they found an empty space where their car had been parked, or more likely another car taking up the space.

He had the radio turned on, but the volume was low. It was tuned to a local station to get an update on the weather, but now the sound was fading and static was breaking up the signal. Impatiently Jimmy twiddled the dial until he found an all-news station, then froze as an announcer's urgent voice reported: "Police have reluctantly confirmed the story broken by station WYME that seven-year-old Brian Dornan, missing since five o'clock this evening, has fallen into the hands of alleged murderer Jimmy Siddons, who is believed to be heading for Canada."

Swearing steadily, Jimmy snapped off the radio. Cally. She must have called the cops. The Thruway's probably already lousy with them, all looking for me—and the kid, he reasoned frantically. He glanced to the left, at the car just passing him. Probably dozens of unmarked cars around here, he thought.

Calm. Keep it calm, he told himself. They didn't know what kind of car he was driving. He wasn't going to be dumb enough to speed or, worse yet, crawl so far below the speed limit that they'd get suspicious.

But the kid was a problem. He had to get rid of him right away. He thought the situation through quickly. He'd get off at the nearest exit, take care of him, dump him fast, and then get back on the road. He looked at the boy sleeping beside him. Too bad, kid, but that's the way it's got to be, he said to himself.

On the right he saw an exit sign. That's it, Jimmy thought, that's the one I'll take.

Brian stirred as though starting to wake up, then fell back asleep. Drowsily, he decided that he must have been dreaming, but he thought he had heard his name.

18

Al Rhodes saw the haunted look on the face of Catherine Dornan when she realized the implications of Brian being with Jimmy Siddons. He watched as she closed her eyes, ready to catch her if she fainted.

But then she opened her eyes quickly and reached out to put her arms around her older son. "We mustn't forget that Brian has the St. Christopher medal," she said softly.

The mask of adult bravado that Michael had managed to maintain throughout the evening's ordeal began to crumble. "I don't want anything to happen to Brian," he sobbed.

Catherine stroked his head. "Nothing is going to happen to him," she said calmly. "Believe that, and hold on to it."

Rhodes could see the effort it took for her to talk. Who the hell leaked to the media that Brian Dornan was with Jimmy Siddons? he wondered angrily. Rhodes could feel his fist itching to connect with the louse who had so thoughtlessly jeopardized the kid's life. His anger was further fed by the realization that if Siddons was listening to the radio, the first thing he'd do was get rid of the boy.

Catherine was saying, "Mother, remember how Dad used to tell us about the Christmas Eve when he was only twenty-two years old and in the thick of the Battle of the Bulge, and he took a couple of soldiers in his company into one of the towns on the fringe of the battle line? Why don't you tell Michael about it?"

Her mother took up the story. "There'd been a report of enemy activity there but it turned out not to be true. On the way back to their battalion, they passed the village church. Midnight Mass had just started. They could see that the church was packed. In the midst of all that fear and danger, everyone had left their homes for the service. Their voices singing 'Silent Night' drifted out into the square. Dad said it was the most beautiful sound he'd ever heard."

Barbara Cavanaugh smiled at her grandson. "Grandpa and the other soldiers went into the church. Grandpa used to tell me how scared all of them had been until they saw the faith and courage of those villagers. Here these people were, surrounded by fierce fighting. They had almost no food. Yet those villagers believed that somehow they'd make it through that terrible time."

Her lower lip quivered, but her voice was steady as she continued. "Grandpa said that was when he *knew* he was going to come home to me. And it was an hour later that the St. Christopher medal kept the bullet from going through his heart."

Catherine looked over Michael's head to Officer Ortiz. "Would you take us to the cathedral now? I want to go to midnight Mass. We'd need to be in a seat where you could find me quickly if you have any news."

"I know the head usher. Ray Hickey," Ortiz said. "I'll take care of it."

She looked at Detective Rhodes. "I will be notified immediately if you have any word at all . . . ?"

"Absolutely." He could not resist adding, "You're very brave, Mrs. Dornan. And I can tell you this for sure: every law enforcement officer in the northeast is dedicated to getting Brian back safely."

"I believe that, and the only way I can help is to pray."

"The leak didn't come from our guys," Mort Levy reported tersely to Chief of Detectives Folney. Apparently some hotshot kid from WYME was watching Cally's apartment and saw us go in, knew something was up, and followed Aika Banks home. He told her he was a cop and pumped her. His name is Pete Cruise."

"Damn good thing it wasn't one of ours. When all this is over, we'll hang Cruise out to dry for impersonating an officer," Folney said. "In the meantime we've got plenty to do here."

He was standing in front of an enlarged map of the northeast that had been attached to the wall of his office. It was crisscrossed with routes outlined in different colors. Folney picked up a pointer. "Here's where we're at, Mort. We've got to assume that Siddons had a car waiting when he left his sister's place. According to her, he left shortly after six. If we're right, and he got in a car immediately, he's been on the road about five and a half hours."

The pointer moved. "The light snow band extends from

the city to about Herkimer, exit 30 on the Thruway. It's heavier throughout New England. But even so, Siddons probably isn't more than four to six hours from the border."

Folney gave a decisive thump to the map. "Amounts to looking for a needle in a haystack."

Mort waited. He knew the boss didn't want comments.

"We've got a special alert along the border," Folney continued. "But with the heavy traffic, he could still be missed, and we all know that someone like Siddons probably knows how to get into Canada without going through a checkpoint." Now he waited for comments.

"How about staging an accident on the major roads to force a one-laner about twenty miles before the border?" Mort suggested.

"I wouldn't rule that out. But on the same principle as erecting a barrier, traffic would build up in two minutes, and Siddons might just try to get off at the nearest exit. If we go ahead with that plan we'll have to put barriers at all the exits, as well."

"And if Siddons feels trapped . . . ?" Mort Levy hesitated. "Siddons has a screw loose, sir. Cally Hunter believes her brother is capable of killing both Brian and himself rather than get captured. I think she knows what she's talking about."

"And if she had had the guts to call us the minute Jimmy left her house with that boy, he wouldn't have gotten out of Manhattan."

Both men turned. Jack Shore was in the doorway. He looked past Mort Levy to Bud Folney. "A new development, sir. A state trooper, Chris McNally, got a hamburger about twenty minutes ago at the travel plaza between Syracuse, exit

39, and Weedsport, exit 40, on the Thruway. He didn't pay much attention at the time, but the woman at the pickup station, a Miss Deidre Lenihan, was talking about a St. Christopher medal that some kid was wearing."

Bud Folney snapped, "Where is the Lenihan woman now?"

"Her shift ended at eleven. Her mother said her boyfriend was picking her up. They're trying to track them down now. But if Cally Hunter had called us earlier none of this would have happened, we could have been at every travel plaza between here and . . ."

Bud Folney almost never raised his voice. But his increasing frustration over the agonizing twists in the manhunt for Jimmy Siddons made him suddenly shout, "Shut up, Jack! 'If only's' don't help now. Do something useful. Get the radio stations in that area to broadcast a plea to Deidre Lenihan to call her mother. Say she's needed at home or something. And for God's sake, don't let anyone connect her to Siddons or that child. Got it?"

19

🌿

From his perch just off the road, Chris McNally kept a watchful eye on the cars passing before him. The snow had finally ended, but the roadway remained icy. At least the drivers were being careful, he thought, although they were all probably frustrated at having to crawl along at thirty-five miles an hour. Since he'd picked up his hamburger, he had only ticketed one driver, a hotshot in a sports car.

Although he was focused on the flow of traffic on the highway, he still could not get his mind off the report of the missing child. The minute the alert had come in about the little boy who was being held hostage by an escaped cop killer, a little boy wearing a St. Christopher medal, Chris had phoned the McDonald's he had just visited and had asked to speak to Deidre Lenihan, the woman who had waited on him. Even though he hadn't really been paying any attention, he remembered that she had been going on about just such a medal and a little boy. Now he was sorry he hadn't been more in the mood to gab with her, especially since they told him she had just left for the evening with her boyfriend.

Despite the tenuous nature of the tip, he nonetheless had reported the possible lead to his supervisor, who had passed it along to One Police Plaza. They had decided it was worth acting on and had asked the local radio station to broadcast an appeal that Deidre call in to police headquarters. From Deidre's mother they had even gotten a description of the boyfriend's car, then they had gotten his license number and put out an all-points call to try and find them.

Deidre's mother had also told them, however, that she thought tonight was going to be special for her daughter, that the boyfriend had let her know his Christmas present was going to be an engagement ring. Chances were they wouldn't be out on the road now, but someplace a little more romantic.

But even if Deidre did hear the radio appeal and did call in, what could she tell them? That she had seen a kid wearing a St. Christopher medal? They knew that already. Did she know the make and model of the car? Had she seen the license plate? From what Chris knew of Deidre, good-hearted as she was, she was not too alert and was observant only when something struck her fancy. No, it was unlikely that she could provide any more significant information.

All of which made Chris even more frustrated. I might have been around that kid myself, he thought. I might have been in line behind them at McDonald's—why didn't I notice anything more?

The thought of having possibly been close to the kidnapped child practically drove him wild. My kids are home in bed right now, he thought. That little boy should be with his family, too. The problem was, he realized, thinking back over his conversation with Deidre, the car with the little boy could have come through there anywhere between a few minutes and an hour before she told him about it. Still, it was the only lead they had, so they had to treat it seriously.

His radio went on. It was headquarters. "Chris," the dispatcher said, "the boss wants to talk to you."

"Sure."

When the captain got on, his voice was urgent. "Chris, the New York City police think your tip is the closest thing they have to a chance of saving that kid's life. We're going to keep on beating the bushes looking for the Lenihan woman, but in the meantime, rack your brain. Try to remember if there was anything else she might have said, anything that might be of some help . . ."

"I'm trying, sir. I'm on the Thruway now. If it's all right with you, I'd like to start driving west. If the guy was on the McDonald's line about the same time as I was, he's got about a ten to fifteen minute lead on me at this point. If I can pick up a little time on him, I'd sure like to be in the vicinity when word does come through from Deidre. I'd like to be there when we get him."

"Okay, go ahead. And, Chris, for God's sake, *think*. Are you sure that she didn't say anything more specific about either the kid with the St. Christopher medal or maybe about the car he was in?"

Just.

The word jumped into Chris's mind. Was it his imagination, or had Deidre said, *"I just saw a kid wearing a St. Christopher medal"*?

He shook his head. He couldn't remember for sure. He did know that the car ahead of him in the line at McDonald's had been a brown Toyota with New York plates.

But there hadn't been a kid in the car, or at least not that he could see. That much he *was* sure of.

Even so . . . if Deidre had said *"just,"* maybe she did mean the Toyota. What had been the license number on that car? He couldn't remember. But he had noticed something about it. What was it?

"Chris?" The supervisor's voice was sharp, effectively breaking his reverie.

"I'm sorry, sir, I was trying to remember. I think Deidre said she had *'just'* seen the kid wearing the medal. If she meant that literally, then it could have been the car directly in front of me on line. That was a brown Toyota with New York plates."

"Do you remember any part of the number?"

"No, I'm just getting a blank. My mind was probably a million miles away."

"And the car, was there definitely a little boy in it?"

"I didn't see one."

"That's not much help. Every third car on the road is probably a Toyota, and tonight they're all so dirty you can't tell one color from another. They probably all look brown."

"No, this one was definitely brown. That much *is* for sure. I just wish I could remember Deidre's exact words."

"Well, don't drive yourself crazy. Let's hope we hear from the Lenihan woman, and in the meantime I'll send one of the other cars to cover your station. Head west. We'll check in later."

At least it feels as if I'm doing something, Chris thought as he signed off, turned the key and pressed his foot on the gas.

The squad car leaped forward. One thing I do know is how to drive, he thought grimly as he steered the vehicle onto the breakdown lane and began passing the cautious motorists along the way.

And as he drove, he continued to try to remember what exactly he had seen in front of him. It was there, imprinted in his mind, he was sure of that. If only he could call it up. As he strained, he felt as though his subconscious were trying to shout out the information. If only he could hear it.

In the meantime, every inch of his six-foot-four-inch being was warning him that time was running out for the missing boy.

Jimmy was seething. What with all the cars going like old ladies were driving them, it had taken him half an hour to get to the nearest exit. Jimmy knew he had to get off the Thruway *now* so he could get rid of the kid. A sign told him he was within a half mile of exit 41 and a town named Waterloo. Waterloo for the kid, he thought with grim satisfaction.

The snow had stopped, but he wasn't sure that was good for him. The slush was turning to ice, and that slowed him up more. Plus, without the snow, it was easier for any cops who might be driving by to get a look at him.

He switched to the right lane. In a minute he'd be able to get off the Thruway. Suddenly the brake lights flashed on the car ahead of him, and Jimmy watched with increasing anger and frustration as the rear of that car fishtailed. "Jerk!" Jimmy screamed. "Jerk! Jerk! Jerk!"

Brian sat up straight, eyes wide open, fully alert. Jimmy began to curse, a steady stream of invective flowing as he realized what had happened. A snowplow four or five cars in front had just switched into the exit lane. Instinctively, he steered the Toyota into the middle lane and barely managed to avoid the fishtailing car. As he pulled abreast of the snowplow, they were just passing the exit.

He slammed the wheel with his fist. Now he'd have to wait till exit 42 to get off the Thruway. How far was that? he wondered.

But as he glanced back at the exit he'd just missed, he realized he actually had been lucky. There was a pileup on the ramp. It must have just happened. That was why the plow had switched lanes. If he had tried to get off there, he could have been stuck for hours.

Finally he saw a sign that informed him the next exit was in six miles. Even at this pace, it shouldn't take more than fifteen minutes. The wheels were gripping the road better. This stretch must have been sanded. Jimmy felt for the gun under his jacket. Should he take it out and hide it under the seat?

No, he decided. If a cop tried to stop him, he needed it just where it was. He glanced at the odometer on the dashboard. He'd set it when he and the kid started driving. It showed that they had gone just over three hundred miles.

There was still a long way to go, but just knowing that he was this close to the Canadian border and Paige was so exciting a sensation he could almost taste it. This time he'd make it work, and whatever he did, this time he wouldn't be dumb enough to be caught by the cops.

Jimmy felt the kid stirring beside him, trying to settle back into sleep. What a mistake! he thought. I should have dumped him five minutes after I took him. I had the car and the money. Why did I think I needed him?

He ached for the moment when he could be rid of the kid and be safe.

20

O fficer Ortiz escorted Catherine, her mother, and Michael to the Fiftieth Street entrance to St. Patrick's Cathedral. A security guard stationed outside was waiting for them. "We have seats for you in the reserved section, ma'am," he told Catherine as he pushed the heavy door open.

The magnificent sound of the orchestra led by the organ and accompanied by the choir filled the great cathedral, which was already packed with worshipers.

"Joyful, joyful," the choir was singing.

Joyful, joyful, Catherine thought. Please God, yes, let this night end like that.

They passed the crèche where the life-sized figures of the Virgin, Joseph, and the shepherds were gathered around the empty pile of hay that was the crib. She knew that the statue of the infant Christ child would be placed there during the Mass.

The security guard showed them to their seats in the sec-

ond row on the middle aisle. Catherine indicated that her
mother should go in first. Then she whispered, "You go between us, Michael." She wanted to be on the outside, at the
end of the row, so she could be aware the minute the door
opened.

Officer Ortiz leaned over. "Mrs. Dornan, if we hear anything, I'll come in for you. Otherwise when Mass is over, the
guard will lead you out first, and I'll be waiting outside in the
car."

"Thank you," Catherine said, then immediately sank to
her knees. The music changed to a swirling pacan of triumph
as the procession began—the choir, the acolytes, deacon,
priests, and bishops, preceding the cardinal, who was carrying the crook of the shepherd in his hand. *Lamb of God*,
Catherine prayed, *please, please save my lamb*.

Chief of Detectives Folney, his gaze still riveted to the map
of the Thruway on the wall of his office, knew that with each
passing minute, the chances of finding Brian Dornan alive
grew slimmer. Mort Levy and Jack Shore were across the
desk from him.

"Canada," he said emphatically. "He's on his way to Canada, and he's getting close to the border."

They had just received further word from Michigan. Paige
Laronde had closed all her bank accounts the day she left
Detroit. And in a burst of confidence, she had told another
dancer that she had been in touch with a guy who was a
genius at creating fake IDs.

It was reported that she had said, "Let me tell you, with
the kind of papers I got for my boyfriend and me, we can
both just *disappear*."

"If Siddons makes it over the border . . ." Bud Folney muttered more to himself than to the others.

"Nothing from the Thruway guys?" he asked for the third time in fifteen minutes.

"Nothing, sir," Mort said quietly.

"Call them again. I want to talk to them myself."

When he got through to Chris McNally's supervisor and heard for himself that absolutely nothing was new, he decided he wanted to speak to Trooper McNally himself.

"A lot of good that'll do," Jack Shore muttered to Mort Levy.

But before Folney could be connected with McNally, another call came in. "Hot lead," an assistant said, rushing into Folney's office. "Siddons and the kid were seen by a trooper about an hour ago at a rest area on Route 91 in Vermont near White River Junction. He said the man matches Siddons's description to a T, and the boy was wearing some kind of medal."

"Forget McNally," Folney said crisply. "I want to talk to the trooper who saw them. And right now, call the Vermont police and have them put up barriers at all the exits north of the sighting. For all we know, the girlfriend may be holed up waiting for him in a farmhouse on this side of the border."

While Folney waited, he looked over at Mort. "Call Cally Hunter and tell her what we've just learned. Ask her if she knows if Jimmy has ever been to Vermont and if so, where did he go? There might be some place in particular he could be headed."

21

Brian could tell that the car was going faster. He opened his eyes, then shut them as fast as he could. It was easier to stay lying down, curled up on the seat, pretending to be asleep, instead of having to try not to act scared when Jimmy looked at him.

He also had been listening to the radio. Even though the volume was turned way down, he could hear what they were saying, that cop killer Jimmy Siddons, who had shot a prison guard, had kidnapped Brian Dornan.

His mother had been reading a book named *Kidnapped* to him and Michael. Brian liked the story a lot, but when they went to bed, Michael told him he thought it was dumb. He had said that if anyone tried to kidnap him, he'd kick the guy and punch him and run away.

Well, I can't run away, Brian thought. And he was sure that trying to hurt Jimmy by punching him wouldn't work. He wished that he'd been able to open the car door earlier and roll out like he had planned to. He'd have curled up in a ball just like they taught the kids to do in gym class. He would have been okay.

But now the car door near him was locked, and he knew that before he could even pull up the lock and open the door, Jimmy would grab him.

Brian was almost crying. He could feel his nose filling up and his eyes getting watery. He tried to think about how Michael might call him a crybaby. Sometimes that helped him when he was trying not to cry.

It didn't help now, though. Even Michael would probably cry if he was scared and he had to go to the bathroom again. And it said right on the radio that Jimmy was dangerous.

But even though he was crying, Brian made sure he didn't make a sound. He felt the tears on his cheeks, but he didn't move to brush them away. If he moved his hand, Jimmy would notice and know he was awake, and for now he had to keep pretending.

Instead, he clasped the St. Christopher medal even tighter and made himself think about how when Dad was able to go back home, they were going to put up their own Christmas tree and open the presents. Just before they had left for New York, Mrs. Emerson who lived next door had come in to say good-bye, and he had heard her say to his mom, "Catherine, no matter when it is, the night you put up your tree, we're all going to come and sing Christmas carols under your window."

Then she'd hugged Brian and said, "I *know* your favorite carol."

"Silent Night." He'd sung it all by himself in the first-grade Christmas pageant at school last year.

Brian tried to sing it to himself now, in his mind . . . but he couldn't get past "Silent night." He knew if he kept thinking about it, he wouldn't be able to keep Jimmy from knowing that he was crying.

Then he almost jumped. Someone on the radio was talking about Jimmy and him again. The man was saying that a state trooper in Vermont was sure he had seen Jimmy Siddons and a young boy in an old Dodge or Chevrolet at a rest stop on Route 91 in Vermont, and the search was being concentrated there.

Jimmy's grim smile vanished as quickly as it had come. The first surge of relief at hearing the news bulletin was followed by instant caution. *Had* some fool claimed he'd spotted them in Vermont? he wondered. It was possible, he decided. When he had been hiding out in Michigan, some two-bit drifter swore he'd seen Jimmy in Delaware. After he got caught at the gas-station job and was taken back to New York, he had found out that the marshals had kept the heat on in Delaware for months.

Even so, being on the Thruway was really beginning to spook him. The road was good and he could make time, but the nearer you got to the border, the more troopers there might be on the road. He decided that when he got off at the next exit, and got rid of the kid, he'd swing over to Route 20. Now that it wasn't snowing, he should be able to make okay time there.

Follow your hunch, Jimmy reminded himself. The only time he hadn't was when he had tried to hold up that gas station. He still remembered that at the time something had warned him there was a problem.

Well, after this, there'll be no more problems, he thought, looking down at Brian. Then when he looked up, he grinned.

The sign looming before him read EXIT 42, GENEVA, ONE MILE AHEAD.

Chris McNally had passed the fender-bender on the exit 41 ramp. Two police cars were on the scene already, so he decided there was no need for him to stop. He had traveled fast, and he hoped that by now he had caught up to any cars that had been ahead of him on line at McDonald's.

Provided, of course, they hadn't taken one of the earlier exits.

A brown Toyota. That's what he kept looking for. Finding it was the one chance. He knew it. What was it about the license plate? He clenched his teeth, again trying hard to remember. There had been something about it . . . Think, damn it, he told himself, *think*.

He didn't for one minute believe the report that Siddons and the kid had been spotted in Vermont. Every gut instinct kept telling Chris that they were nearby.

Exit 42 to Geneva was coming up. That meant the border was only another hundred miles or so away. Most of the cars were doing fifty to sixty miles an hour now. If Jimmy Siddons was in this vicinity, he could look forward to being out of the country in less than two hours.

What was there about the license plate of the Toyota? he asked himself once more.

Chris's eyes narrowed. He could see a dark Toyota in the passing lane that was moving fast. He switched lanes and drove up beside it, then glanced in. He prayed that it held a single man or a man with a young boy. Just a chance to find that child. Give me a chance, he prayed.

Without turning on his siren or dome light, Chris continued past the Toyota. He had been able to see a young couple inside. The guy was driving with his arm around the girl, not a good idea on an icy road. Another time he'd have pulled him over.

Chris stepped on the gas. The road was clearer, the traffic was better spaced. But everything was moving faster and faster, and closer and closer to Canada.

His radio was on low when a call came in for him. "Officer McNally?"

"Yes."

"New York City Chief of Detectives Bud Folney calling you from One Police Plaza. I just spoke to your supervisor again. The Vermont sighting is a washout. The Lenihan woman can't be found. Tell me what you reported earlier about a brown Toyota."

Knowing his boss had dismissed that, Chris realized that this Folney must be really pressing him.

He explained that if Deidre had been talking about the car directly ahead of him in the McDonald's line, she was talking about a brown Toyota with New York plates.

"And you can't remember the license."

"No, sir." Chris wanted to strangle the words in his throat. "But there was something unusual about it."

He was almost at exit 42. As he watched, a vehicle two cars ahead switched into the exit lane. His casual glance became a stare. "My God," he said.

"Officer? What is it?" In New York, Bud Folney instinctively knew that something was happening.

"That's it." Chris said. "It wasn't the license plate I no-

ticed. It was the bumper sticker. There's just a piece of it left and it says *inheritance*. Sir, I'm following that Toyota down the exit ramp right now. Can you check out the license?"

"Don't lose that car," Bud snapped. "And hang on."

Three minutes later the phone rang in apartment 8C, in 10 Stuyvesant Oval, in lower Manhattan. A sleepy and anxious Edward Hillson picked it up. "Hello," he said. He felt his wife's nervous grasp on his arm.

"What? My car? I parked it around the corner at five or so. No, I didn't lend it to anyone. Yes. It's a brown Toyota. What are you telling me?"

Bud Folney got back to Chris. "I think you have him, but for God's sake remember, he's threatened to kill the child before he lets himself get captured. So be careful."

22

ichael was so sleepy. All he wanted to do was lean against Gran and close his eyes. But he couldn't do that yet, not until he was sure that Brian was okay. Michael struggled to suppress his growing fear. *Why didn't he grab me if he saw that lady pick up Mom's wallet? I could have run after her and helped him when he got caught by that guy.*

The cardinal was at the altar now. But when the music stopped, instead of starting to offer Mass, he began to speak. "On this night of joy and hope . . ."

Off to the right, Michael could see the television cameras. He had always thought it would be cool to be on television, but whenever he had thought about it, the circumstances he envisioned had to do with winning something or with witnessing some great event. That would be fun. Tonight, when he and Mom were on together, it wasn't fun.

It was awful to hear Mom begging people to help them find Brian.

". . . in a year that has brought so much violence to the innocent . . ."

Michael straightened up. The cardinal was talking about them, about Dad being sick and Brian being missing and believed to be with that escaped killer. He was saying, "Brian Dornan's mother, grandmother, and ten-year-old brother are with us at this Mass. Let our special prayer be that Dr. Thomas Dornan will recover fully and that Brian will be found unharmed."

Michael could see that Mom and Gran were both crying. Their lips were moving, and he knew they were praying. His prayer was the advice he would have given Brian if he could hear him: *Run, Brian, run.*

Now that he was off the Thruway, Jimmy felt somewhat relieved, despite a gnawing sense that things were closing in on him.

He was running low on gas but was afraid to risk stopping at a station with the kid in the car. He was on Route 14 south. That connected with Route 20 in about six miles. Route 20 led to the border.

There was a lot less traffic here than on the Thruway. Most people were home by now anyway, asleep or getting ready for Christmas morning. It was unlikely that anyone would be looking for him here. Still, he reasoned, the best thing to do was to get on some of the local streets in Geneva, find someplace like a school where there'd be a parking lot, or find a wooded area, somewhere he could stop without being noticed and do what he had to do.

As he took the next right-hand turn, he glanced in the rearview mirror. His antennae went up. He thought he had seen headlights reflected there as he made the turn, but now he didn't see them anymore.

I'm getting too jumpy, he thought.

A block later it suddenly was like they'd sailed off the edge of the earth. As far as he could see, there were no cars ahead. They were in a residential area, quiet and dark. The houses were mostly unlit, except some of them still had Christmas-tree lights glowing from bushes and evergreens on the snow-covered lawns.

He couldn't be sure if the kid was really asleep or faking it. Not that it mattered. This was the sort of place he needed. He drove six blocks and then saw what he was looking for: a school, with a long driveway that had to lead to a parking area.

His eyes missed nothing as he carefully searched the area for any sign of an approaching car or someone out walking. Then he stopped the car and opened the window halfway, listening intently for any hint of trouble. The cold instantly turned his breath to steam. He could hear nothing but the hum of the Toyota's engine. It was quiet out there. Silent.

Still, he decided to drive around the block one more time, just to be sure he wasn't being followed.

As he put his foot on the accelerator, and as the car slowly moved forward, he kept his gaze glued to the rearview mirror. Damn. He'd been right. There *was* a car behind him, running without lights. Now it was moving, too. The lights from a brilliantly lit tree reflected on its rooftop dome.

A squad car. Cops! Damn them, Jimmy swore under his breath. Damn them! Damn them! He tromped on the gas pedal. It might be his last ride, but he'd make it a good one.

He looked down at Brian. "Quit pretending. I know you're

awake," he shouted. "Sit up, damn you. I shoulda ditched you as soon as I was out of the city. Lousy kid."

Jimmy floored the accelerator. A quick look in the rear-view mirror confirmed that the pursuing car had also speeded up and was now openly following him. But so far there seemed to be only one of them.

Clearly Cally had told the cops he had the kid, he reasoned. She'd probably also told them that he said he'd kill the kid first if they tried to close in on him. If that cop behind him knew that, it explained why he wasn't trying to pull him over right now.

He glanced at the speedometer: fifty . . . sixty . . . seventy. Damn this car! Jimmy thought, suddenly wishing he had something more powerful than a Toyota. He hunched over the wheel. He couldn't outrun them, but he still might have a chance to get away.

The guy chasing him didn't have backup yet. What would he do if he saw the kid had been shot and pushed out of the car? He'd stop to try to help him, Jimmy reasoned. I'd better do it right away, he thought, before he has time to call in help.

He reached inside his jacket for his gun. Just then the car hit a patch of ice and began to skid. Jimmy dropped the gun in his lap, turned the wheels in the direction of the skid, then managed to straighten the car just inches away from crashing into a tree at the edge of the sidewalk.

Nobody can drive like I can, he thought grimly. Then he picked up the gun again and released the safety catch. If the cop stops for the kid, I'll make it to Canada, he promised himself. He released the lock on the passenger door and reached across the terrified boy to open it.

23

Cally knew she had to call police headquarters to see if there was any word about little Brian. She had told Detective Levy she didn't think Jimmy would try to reach Canada through Vermont. "He got in trouble up there when he was about fifteen," she'd said. "He never did time there, but I think some sheriff really scared Jimmy. He told him he had a long memory and warned him never to show up in Vermont again. Even though that was at least ten years ago, Jimmy is superstitious. I think he'd stick to the Thruway. I know he went to Canada a couple of times when he was a teenager, and both times he went that way."

Levy had listened to her. She knew he wanted to trust her, and she prayed that this time he had. She also prayed that she was right and they got the boy back safely, so she could know that in some small way she had helped.

Someone other than Levy answered his phone, and she was told to wait. Then Levy came on. "What is it, Cally?"

"I just had to know if there's been any word . . . I've been praying that what I told you about Jimmy taking the Thruway helped."

Levy's voice softened even though he still spoke quickly. "Cally, it did help, and we're very grateful. I can't talk now, but whatever prayers you know, keep saying them."

That means they must have located Jimmy, she thought. But what was happening to Brian?

Cally sank to her knees. *It doesn't matter what happens to me*, she prayed. *Stop Jimmy before he hurts that child.*

Chris McNally had known it the minute Jimmy spotted him. The radio was open between him and headquarters and was tied in to One Police Plaza in Manhattan. "He knows he's being followed," Chris reported tersely. "He's taking off like a bat out of hell."

"Don't lose him," Bud Folney said quietly.

"We've got a dozen cars on the way, Chris," the dispatcher snapped. "They're running silent and on dim lights. They'll surround you. We're bringing in a chopper, too."

"Keep them out of sight!" Chris pressed his foot on the accelerator. "He's going seventy. There's not many cars out, but these streets aren't completely cleared. This is getting dangerous."

As Siddons raced across an intersection, Chris watched in horror as he barely missed slamming into another car. Siddons was driving like a maniac. There was going to be an accident, he knew it. "Passing Lakewood Avenue," he reported. Two blocks later he saw the Toyota skid and almost hit a tree. A minute after that, he yelled, "The boy!"

"What is it?" Folney demanded.

"The passenger door of the Toyota just opened. The inside light's on, so I can see the kid struggling. Oh God . . . Siddons has his gun out. It looks like he's going to shoot him."

24

"*Kyrie Eleison*," the choir sang.
    Lord have mercy, Barbara Cavanaugh prayed.
    Save my lamb, Catherine begged.
  Run, Dork, run, get away from him, Michael shouted in his mind.

Jimmy Siddons was crazy. Brian had never been in a car before that was going so fast. He wasn't sure what was going on, but there must be someone following them.

Brian looked away from the road for a moment and glanced at Jimmy. He had his gun out. He felt Jimmy tugging at his seat belt, releasing it. Then he reached across Brian and opened the door beside him. He could feel the cold air rushing in.

For a moment he was paralyzed with fear. Then he sat up very straight. He realized what was about to happen. That Jimmy was going to shoot him and push him out of the car.

He had to get away. He was still clutching the medal in his right hand. He felt Jimmy poke him in the side with the gun, pushing him toward the open door and the roadway rushing beneath them. Holding onto the seat-belt buckle with his left hand, he swung out blindly with his right. The medal arced and slammed into Jimmy's face, catching him in his left eye.

Jimmy yelled and took his hand off the wheel, instinctively slamming his foot on the brake. As he grabbed his eye, the gun went off. The bullet whistled past Brian's ear as the out-of-control car began to spin around. It jumped the curb, went up into a corner lawn, and caught on a bush. Still spinning, it slowed as it dragged the bush back across the lawn and out onto the edge of the road.

Jimmy was swearing now, one hand again on the wheel, the other aiming the gun. Blood dripped into his eye from a gash across his forehead and cheek.

Get out. Get out. Brian heard the command in his head as though someone were shouting it at him. Brian dove for the door and rolled out onto the snow-covered lawn just as a second bullet passed over his shoulder.

"Jesus Christ, the kid's out of the car," Chris yelled. He jammed on the brakes and skidded to a stop behind the Toyota. "He's getting up. Oh my God."

Bud Folney shouted, "Is he hurt?" but Chris didn't hear him. He was already out of his car and running toward the boy. Siddons was in control of the Toyota again and had turned it, clearly planning to run over Brian. In what seemed like an eternity but was actually only seconds, Chris had crossed the space between him and Brian and gathered the boy in his arms.

The car was racing toward them, its passenger door still open and its interior still illuminated so that the maniacal anger in Jimmy Siddons's face was clearly visible. Clutching

Brian tightly against him, Chris dove to the side and rolled down a snowy incline just as the wheels of the Toyota passed inches from their heads. An instant later, with a sickening sound of metal crashing and glass breaking, the vehicle careened off the porch of the house and flipped over.

For a moment there was silence, and then the quiet was shattered as sirens screamed and wailed. Lights from a dozen squad cars brightened the night as swarms of troopers raced to surround the overturned vehicle. Chris lay in the snow for a few seconds, hugging Brian to him, listening to the convergence of sounds. Then he heard a small relieved voice ask, "Are you St. Christopher?"

"No, but right now I feel like him, Brian," Chris said heartily. "Merry Christmas, son."

25

Officer Manuel Ortiz slipped noiselessly through the side door of the cathedral and instantly caught Catherine's eye. He smiled and nodded his head. She jumped up and ran to meet him.

"Is he . . ."

"He's fine. They're sending him back in a police helicopter. He'll be here by the time Mass is over."

Noticing that one of the television cameras was trained on them, Ortiz raised his hand and made a circle of his thumb and forefinger, a symbol that for this moment, on this most special of days, everything was A-OK.

Those seated nearby witnessed the exchange and began to clap softly. As others turned, they stood, and applause began to slowly rumble through the giant cathedral. It was a full five minutes before the deacon could begin to read the Christmas Gospel, " 'And it came to pass . . .' "

• • •

"I'm going to let Cally know what's happened," Mort Levy told Bud Folney. "Sir, I know she should have called us earlier, but I hope . . ."

"Don't worry. I'm not going to play Scrooge tonight. She worked with us. She deserves a break," Folney said crisply. "Besides, the Dornan woman has already said she's not going to press charges against her." He paused for a moment, thinking. "Listen, there's got to be some toys left in the station houses. Tell the guys to get busy and round some up for that little girl of Cally's. Have them meet us at Cally's building in forty-five minutes. Mort, you and I are going to give them to her. Shore, you go home."

It was Brian's first helicopter ride, and even though he was incredibly tired, he was too excited to even think about closing his eyes. He was sorry Officer McNally—Chris, as he had said he should call him—hadn't been able to come with him. But he had been with Brian when they took Jimmy Siddons away, and he had told him not to worry, that this was one guy who would never get out of prison again. And then he'd gotten the St. Christopher medal out of the car for Brian.

As the helicopter came down it looked like it was almost landing on the river. He recognized the Fifty-ninth Street Bridge and the Roosevelt Island tramway. His dad had taken him for a ride on that. He wondered suddenly if his father knew what had happened to him.

He turned to one of the officers. "My dad's in a hospital near here. I have to go see him. He might be worried."

The officer, who was by now familiar with the story of the whole Dornan family, said, "You'll see him soon, son. But now, your mother's waiting for you. She's at midnight Mass at St. Patrick's Cathedral."

When the buzzer sounded at Cally's Avenue B apartment, she answered it with the resigned belief that she was going to be arrested. Detective Levy had called to say only that he and another officer were coming by. But it was two beaming, self-appointed Santa Clauses who arrived at her door, laden with dolls and games and a sparkling white wicker doll's carriage.

As she watched, unbelieving, they placed the gifts under and around the Christmas tree.

"Your information about your brother was a tremendous help," Bud Folney said. "The Dornan boy is okay and on his way back to the city. Jimmy is on his way back to prison; he's our responsibility once again, and I promise we won't let him get away this time. From now on I hope it gets a lot better for you."

Cally felt as though a giant weight had been lifted from her. She could only whisper, "Thank you . . . thank you . . ."

Folney and Levy chorused, "Merry Christmas, Cally," and were gone.

When they left, Cally at last knew she could go to bed and sleep. Gigi's even breathing was an answered prayer. From now on, she'd be able to hear it every night, and listen without fear that her little girl would be taken away from her again. Everything *will* get better, she thought. I know it now.

As she fell asleep, her last thought was that when Gigi saw that the big package with Santa's present was missing from under the Christmas tree, she could honestly tell her that Santa Claus had come and taken it away.

· · ·

The recessional was about to start when once again the side door of the cathedral opened and Officer Ortiz entered. This time he was not alone. He bent down to the small boy beside him and pointed. Before Catherine could get to her feet, Brian was in her arms, the St. Christopher medal he was wearing pressed against her heart.

As she held him close, she said nothing, but felt the silent tears of relief and joy course down her cheeks, knowing that he once again was safe, and firm in her belief now that Tom was going to make it, too.

Barbara also did not speak, but leaned over and laid her hand on her grandson's head.

It was Michael who broke the silence with whispered words of welcome. "Hi, Dork," he said with a grin.

Christmas Day

Christmas morning dawned cold and clear. At ten o'clock, Catherine, Brian, and Michael arrived at the hospital.

Dr. Crowley was waiting for them when they got off the elevator on the fifth floor. "My God, Catherine," he said, "are you okay? I hadn't heard about what happened until I got here this morning. You must be exhausted."

"Thanks, Spence, but I'm fine." She looked at her sons. "We're all fine. But how is Tom? When I called this morning, all they would say was that he had a good night."

"And he did. It's an excellent sign. He had a very good night. A lot better than yours, that's for sure. I hope you don't mind, but I decided it was best if I told Tom about Brian. The press have been calling here all morning, and I didn't want to risk his hearing about it from an outsider. When I told him, I started with the happy ending, of course."

Catherine felt relief rush through her. "I'm glad he knows, Spence. I didn't know how to tell him. I couldn't be sure how he'd take it."

"He took it very well, Catherine. He's a lot stronger than you might think." Crowley looked at the medal around Brian's neck. "I understand you went through a lot to make sure you'd be able to give that medal to your dad. I promise all of you that between St. Christopher and me, we'll make sure he gets well."

The boys tugged at Catherine's hands.

"He's waiting for you," Spence said, smiling.

The door of Tom's room was partly open. Catherine pushed it the rest of the way and stood looking at her husband.

The head of the bed was elevated. When Tom saw them, his face brightened with that familiar smile.

The boys ran to him, then carefully stopped just inches from the bed. They both reached out and grasped his hand. Catherine watched his eyes fill with tears when he looked at Brian.

He's so pale, she thought. I can tell that he hurts. But he *is* going to get better. She did not need to force the radiant smile that her lips formed as Michael lifted the chain with the St. Christopher medal from Brian's neck and together they put it on Tom. "Merry Christmas, Dad," they chorused.

As her husband looked over their sons' heads and his lips formed the words *I love you*, other words sang through Catherine's being.

All is calm . . . all is bright.

POCKET
B O O K S

STILLWATCH

MARY HIGGINS CLARK

Top investigative journalist Pat Traymore is in
Washington, finding out everything she can about
Abigail Jennings, the ambitious but highly
secretive Senator tipped to be the first woman
Vice-President.

Pat has another, deeply personal reason for being
in Washington. As a child she suffered a
horrifying experience which left her badly hurt,
and both her parents dead. Now, tormented by
painful snatches of memory, she finds herself
back in the old house which has the power to
reveal secrets she thought long-buried.

And as her search for truth unleashes powerful
and menacing forces against her, it looks as if the
present may turn out to be even more terrifying
than the past.

PRICE £5.99

ISBN 0 671 85397 X

POCKET
B O O K S

WEEP NO MORE, MY LADY

MARY HIGGINS CLARK

Beautiful young Elizabeth Lange is haunted by the tragic loss of her beloved sister, Leila - a stage and screen star who plunged to her death form the balcony of her New York penthouse. But the circumstances are mysterious. Why would Leila take her own life at the height of her fame and success?

Invited to Cypress Point Spa by a friend, Elizabeth finds herself confronted by a cast of characters who all had motives for killing her sister - including Leila's lover, Ted Winters. And she quickly discovers her own life might also be under threat ...

PRICE £5.99

ISBN 0 671 85399 6

POCKET
B O O K S

LET ME CALL YOU SWEETHEART

MARY HIGGINS CLARK

When Kerry McGrath - a smart, relentless
prosecutor - takes her daughter to see a plastic
surgeon following a car accident, she sees a
woman in the surgery with a beautiful,
hauntingly familiar face. On a subsequent visit,
she sees the same face again - on a different
woman . . .

Suddenly she remembers: both these women look
startlingly like Suzanne Reardon, the 'Sweetheart
Murder' victim whose husband, Skip, is now
serving a life sentence for that murder.

When Kerry starts asking questions, she discovers
that just about everyone wants to keep the case
closed. Still she persists - but her puzzled queries
have triggered a response and she finds herself in
great, growing danger.

PRICE £5.99

ISBN 0 671 85347 3

POCKET
B O O K S

This book and other **Mary Higgins Clark** titles are available from your book shop or can be ordered direct from the publisher.

0 671 01039 5	**Before I Say Goodbye**	£5.99
0 671 01038 7	**We'll Meet Again**	£5.99
0 671 02284 9	**All Through the Night**	£4.99
0 671 01037 9	**You Belong to Me**	£5.99
0 671 00503 0	**Pretend You Don't See Her**	£5.99
0 671 00504 9	**My Gal Sunday**	£5.99
0 671 85348 1	**Moonlight Becomes You**	£5.99
0 671 85397X	**Stillwatch**	£4.99
0 671 85347 3	**Let Me Call You Sweetheart**	£5.99
0 671 85345 7	**Remember Me**	£4.99
0 671 85399 6	**Weep No More My Lady**	£4.99
0 671 85396 1	**A Cry in the Night**	£5.99
0 671 85394 5	**The Cradle Will Fall**	£5.99
0 671 85395 3	**A Stranger is Watching**	£4.99

Please send cheque or postal order for the value of the book, free postage and packing within the UK; OVERSEAS including Republic of Ireland £1 per book.

OR: Please debit this amount from my

VISA/ACCESS/MASTERCARD..

CARD NO:..

EXPIRY DATE...

AMOUNT£..

NAME..

ADDRESS...

....

SIGNATURE..

Send orders to SIMON & SCHUSTER CASH SALES
PO Box 29, Douglas Isle of Man, IM99 1BQ
Tel: 01624 836000, Fax: 01624 670923
www.bookpost.co.uk
Please allow 14 days for delivery. Prices and availability subject to
change without notice